D0379086

ALSO BY

AMARA LAKHOUS

Clash of Civilizations Over an Elevator in Piazza Vittorio

Divorce Islamic Style

DISPUTE OVER A VERY ITALIAN PIGLET

Amara Lakhous

DISPUTE OVER A VERY ITALIAN PIGLET

Translated from the Italian
by Ann Goldstein

Europa Editions
214 West 29th Street
New York, N.Y. 10001
www.europaeditions.com
info@europaeditions.com

First Publication 2014 by Europa Editions

Translation by Ann Goldstein
Original title: *Contesa per un maialino italianissimo a San Salvario*

Library of Congress Cataloging in Publication Data is available
ISBN 978-1-60945-188-2

Lakhous, Amara
Dispute Over a Very Italian Piglet

Book design by Emanuele Ragnisco
www.mekkanografici.com

Cover illustration by Chiara Carrer

Prepress by Grafica Punto Print – Rome

Printed in the USA

For Stephanie

Mr. Editor, you show these southerners too much respect by taking an interest in them in your noble, long-established newspaper. As far as I'm concerned, there is no "question of the southerners in Turin" but only the problem of sending home shirkers and good-for-nothings, who come to the north not to work but only to commit crimes. Send them back to their land, and let that be the end of it.

Gazzetta del Popolo, November, 1959

I am a southerner, married, with a child a few months old. I ask no favors, only an apartment to rent, and I can give the highest guarantee of payment. I buy *La Stampa* every day, and I read with pleasure some article or item of news, good or bad, and finally my gaze falls on the classified ads. Even though I bombard the advertisers with telephone calls all day, starting early in the morning, I always find the line busy, and if someone should happen to answer, the first question I get is the following: "You're a southerner? I'm sorry, I can't." Or other responses too repellent to repeat, or perhaps, "Our rooms are quiet, and we don't want the disturbances that children cause." Since I don't have the privilege of at least explaining myself, and since as soon as I'm identified as a southerner the excuse of the children comes up, I would like to address a few words to these people who are more civilized than me: I am and feel myself a Christian, and so I believe that all of us in the world are children of God. In all the nations of the world, without distinction between north and south, there are good people and bad, with children and without children. I personally deplore these ways of thinking: How can we celebrate the Centenary of Italian Unification with such feelings?

La Stampa, June 21, 1961

CONTENTS

DISPUTE OVER A VERY ITALIAN PIGLET

Chapter 1
Neither Here Nor There

I get out of bed with my eyes closed and move toward the window like a blind man without a cane. I part the curtains and slowly open the blinds. Voices and other sounds caress my ears. I feel a shiver on my skin. I wait a few seconds, then, suddenly, I open my eyes: there before me, in all its splendor, is the Vieux-Port.

I stand there, admiring the beauty of this October light, child of sun and sea. I look at the fishermen's stalls, I extend my gaze farther out, to the boats moving away from the port. I become aware of Taina's presence beside me, I feel her fingers on my back. Her hair, still a little wet, dazzles me. Now there is too much light. I sniff the freshness of her body. I kiss her gently on the neck, but Taina senses the trap and disentangles herself like a clever prey.

"Enzo, stop it! I have to go. The taxi's waiting downstairs."

"What's the rush?"

"You'll make me miss the plane to Helsinki."

"Just a kiss."

Taina grants me a passionate French kiss and escapes. Such a pity, the time we have is never generous. The hours pass quickly. We've been in Marseilles for three days but it feels as if we'd arrived only yesterday.

I met Taina, the jewel of my conquests, in peculiar circumstances, a year and a half ago, at the Porta Nuova station in Turin. That initial encounter was unforgettable: a gorgeous blonde who was crying desperately, because her suitcase had been stolen. At first sight, she appeared to be a foreign tourist, but in fact she was in the city for work. I stepped in without thinking twice. Evidently I hadn't lost my habit of sticking my nose in other people's business. What can I do? I like helping people, the way a doctor or a fireman does. It took some time to calm her down. If I could have embraced her that would have been a big help, but it couldn't be done, I'd never seen her before. So I contented myself with a few routine phrases. The truth is that this beautiful Finnish woman had really screwed up. She had in the suitcase not only clothes but documents and, most crucial, a really important contract for Nokia—she's the company's European representative. She risked being fired. I went with her first to the police station near Porta Nuova to make a report, then to the hotel near Piazza San Carlo where she usually stayed. Luckily the guy at the desk proved to be understanding and didn't make a fuss about the documents. Taina was a regular guest, and, besides, she was generous with tips, so all she had to do was tell him about the lost suitcase. I left her less desperate than before. Maybe she was ready to resign herself. As I said goodbye, I promised I'd get busy and recover the suitcase. And I consider a promise sacred.

Coming out of the hotel I had a wicked idea, of the type that I find extremely amusing. I called an old acquaintance, Franco, who's known as Tamburo, the Drum. Besides being crazy about drums of all kinds, which explains the origin of his nickname, he is also a baronet among Turin's thieves and fences. I told him that a suitcase belonging to the Security Services had been stolen at the station an hour earlier and that some informer, probably one of his colleagues, had dragged his name into it. And, to be precise and get to the point, I added that the suitcase belonged to a blonde who was working undercover. I didn't have to continue the story. Tamburo got the gist immediately; he has a good memory. A year earlier, he had had a nasty experience with the Services. He had been commissioned by "someone" to steal the laptop of a Russian diplomat visiting Piedmont. Top-secret documents were involved. The operation didn't have a good outcome. He was caught like an amateur. How was he supposed to know that the diplomat was in fact a KGB agent, a really sharp son of a bitch? Besides, when things go wrong it's always the weakest who pay the bill. Tamburo took all the blame, to protect his bosses. He did a few months in jail, spending a lot of money out of his own pocket for a famous lawyer. So the theft of Taina's suitcase might sound to him like a serious blunder. A blunder leads to revenge and revenge does harm and makes noise. This our Tamburo absolutely did not want. His business requires total silence. We understood each other without too much beating about the bush: it's better to find "the suitcase belonging to the Security Services" and give it back right away—otherwise there's trouble. Tamburo hadn't lost the old habit of swearing on the head of his son, and this made me angry. Children should be left in peace, they shouldn't be used as pawns.

For my part, I was sure of one thing: if it wasn't him personally who had stolen the suitcase, it must have been someone he knew. There are no professional secrets in this line of work. A simple theory, which, however, always holds true. In the end, though, he asked for a little time to investigate; I felt like I was talking to the Turin chief of police himself.

After a couple of hours he called, saying that he had found the suitcase, untouched. What a guy! He asked me the favor of acting as middleman to give it back. Why? He wished to remain "outside this business that smells like shit." Those were his actual words. That is, not a shitty business but a business that smells like shit. Tamburo wanted to keep both his ass and his nose clean. Can you blame him? To puff myself up a bit, I said, before agreeing, that I would do it, but just to keep him out of trouble. He thanked me effusively. I was satisfied; I had already reserved a favor for the future. You never know, life is full of emergencies. A Tamburo can always be useful.

A few minutes later we were in San Salvario, near my house, for the handover. Tamburo was very nervous, trembling like a dry leaf. He looked over his shoulder, fearful he'd been followed. I listened to his load of nonsense reluctantly: I'm finished with the criminal life, I'm another person now, I don't want trouble, I want to set a good example for my son, blah blah blah. The usual bullshit of fucking criminals who aren't ever sorry. I left him terrified. I'm sure he didn't sleep that night.

A little before midnight I myself, in a state of complete euphoria, was at the reception desk of the hotel with the suitcase belonging to the Security Services. To tell the truth, I felt rather like Alexander the Great, Napoleon Bonaparte, or Giuseppe Garibaldi triumphantly entering a newly conquered city. Taina was really happy. She glanced quickly through the suitcase: nothing missing. Probably because she was tired, she didn't even ask how I had managed to find it. With a seductive look and that Nordic accent that makes us poor fellows see the sun at midnight and the moon at noon she said to me:

"I don't know how to thank you."

"There's just one way."

"What?"

"Accept my invitation to dinner tomorrow."

"I'm sorry, I leave tomorrow at noon, but I'll be back in Turin in two weeks. I'll call you."

"OK."

OK like hell! I left with a handshake, not even a kiss on the cheek! Northerners, as everyone knows, are very formal. Not like us Italians, Mediterranean, uninhibited, with all our kisses, hugs, pats on the shoulder, and various other kinds of touching. So I had to be content with her card. I, however, never having had a goddam card, gave her my cell phone number. What could I do? It wasn't the moment to insist. In fact I felt like a real halfwit, the king of jerks. I should at least have tried. What the hell! I had a chance. Did I save her from being fired, yes or no? Did I find her documents, yes or no? Did I give her back her clothes, yes or no? Did I spare her a restless, sleepless night, yes or no? Did I deserve a reward, yes or no? But I gave in without a whimper. Disgraceful! What had the Latin lover come to? For a few days I sharply regretted it. But luckily Taina was as good as her word. Two weeks later she was back, and she remembered me. That same night our more than intimate relationship began. I didn't do much. It was she who led the game from the start. I merely invited her to my house for a *risotto alla Laganà* and a glass of red wine from the Piedmont, a Nebbiolo.

Now, riveted to the spot, I stare at the Vieux-Port, thinking of my situation as a single man. I admit it's a choice, not forced. Why complain? I'm like that. I'm not keen on long relationships. I can't bear routine—it takes courage to play the same part for days, weeks, months, even years. My sister Paola maintains that I need a therapist (a female one would be best), to cure my "woman-phobia." Maybe she's right, maybe not. While I'm waiting for psychological improvement I continue to believe that being part of a couple is not my cup of tea. This is what my sainted mother can't understand: "Enzù, my son, time waits for no man. You see, you'll end up alone! You've got to get married and have children." Mamma, what's the rush to have a stranger in the house, as the great Alberto Sordi once said.

I take an orange juice from the minifridge, a pack of MS cigarettes, a.k.a. *morte sicura*, certain death, and my cell phone, and go out to sit on the little balcony and enjoy the sun. The Vieux-Port is slowly emptying as the fishermen pack up their stalls. I light the first cigarette and take a deep drag. I glance at the phone to see what time it is. God damn! Thirty calls and no answer. What happened. I don't have time to find out the origin of the calls when here comes another.

"Enzo, it's Maritani. Finally! I've been looking for you since this morning."

"Sorry, I had the sound turned down."

"Where the hell are you? How can you not know? We've got a real mess here."

"What happened?"

"Are you kidding? Where are you living? On Mars? In ten minutes we'll have the third briefing of the day. I've got nothing on the murder of those Albanians last night, apart from the sweet bit of news that some of them were found with their genitals in their mouths! You make me look like an idiot, a shit editor! You think I'm a dickhead?"

"Come on."

"I want you at the office immediately."

"I can't now."

"What do you mean you can't?"

"I've been following a lead since this morning. I need time, Angelo."

"What lead? We know that the Albanians, two men and two women, were killed in three different places in Turin. The method was the same? Is that it? Can you give me something?"

"I can't now. I'll explain everything later."

"Do you have a source, Enzo?"

"Yes. Let's say that . . . "

Voilà! Les jeux sont faits! The eggs are broken.

"A Deep Throat. Is that it?"

"Yes."

"I'll call you later, all right? Where are you now?"

"I'm in Mar . . . in Marconi."

Basically it's not so hard to pretend to be in Corso Marconi in San Salvario while you're looking at the Vieux-Port of

Marseilles! All you need is nerve and serious balls. That's it. Now, however, I have a hot potato on my hands. Rather, four. The number of murdered Albanians. Is it revenge? Maybe. Here I have to make something up. I told Maritani that I had a trail, a Deep Throat, to be exact. I can't go back. This business of the deep throat pisses me off. My editor is a real romantic, for want of a less elegant adjective. He's still thinking about the Nixon investigation in '74. Try to convince Maritani that Watergate was a setup. A story of settling scores, as usual. A human vendetta. It was Mark Felt, with that comic-book name, the No. 2 in the F.B.I., who revealed to Bob Woodward and Carl Bernstein Nixon's maneuvers against his Democratic opponents. Felt, alias Deep Throat, came out into the open only last year. I ask myself: what great thing did the two reporters do? They were simply used as pawns to fuck poor Nixon! Let's summarize: Felt aims at the job of No. 1 in the F.B.I. after the death of the old, feared J. Edgar Hoover in 1972, the people in the White House choose someone else, he gets his revenge, by exposing his enemies. All clear?

There are no scoops without tips, without anonymous sources, it's the first real rule of journalism I learned. I'm allergic to colleagues who transform themselves into heroes, myths, or, even worse, martyrs. Should I be getting nervous? No, absolutely. It's not worth it. I have to think of a lead, but not right away. I still have some time. I'd like to take my afternoon walk in tranquility. The sun in Marseilles is stupendous, the sea makes me truly happy. I'll have to leave tomorrow, ahead of time—I can't stay till Tuesday. Alas! I'll have to leave beautiful Marseilles and go back to Turin. This Albanian trouble requires my physical presence at the crime scenes. I can't manage it from outside. I call my friend Jean-Pierre to tell him about the change of plan and try to reschedule our dinner for tonight.

I have lunch around two at a bistro near the hotel, where I sit on the terrace to enjoy the panorama of the Vieux-Port. I order a salad Niçoise and a glass of red wine. My dinner with Jean-Pierre is set for eight at his house, in the Panier district. So there's time for a good walk. After my meal, I feel like having an Arab mint tea in the North African neighborhood. There's a small casbah near the intersection of Rue de la Canebière and Rue de Rome. The neighborhood, called Noailles, is famous for its Arab market, which is very crowded on weekends. It resembles our market in Porta Palazzo. I go into a shop that sells Arab pastries, and where you can also get mint tea. The aromas are intense, and there's a Tunisian pastry I can never resist, called *zlabia*. It's fried and very sweet, made with honey. Luckily I don't suffer from diabetes or ulcers, so I can indulge.

I return to the Vieux-Port, and decide to go to the cathedral of Notre-Dame de la Garde. I like seeing Marseilles from high up. There's a very convenient way to get there, in a vehicle that's a cross between a train, a minibus, a mechanical worm, and a gigantic toy. It would drive all the children in the world mad. There are three seats in each row. Only tourists use it. In Marseilles I'm often taken for a North African. Let's just say that I have an Arab-looking face. Taina finds it very amusing to make fun of me by calling me "Mohamed" when we go to an Arab restaurant; that way, she explains, they'll treat us with the proper respect. Taina is a genius of marketing.

I've been coming to France for some twenty years; I'm very fond of Paris and, even more, of Marseilles. I think Turin is a perfect blend of Paris and Marseilles. Learning French was easy, since it's not that different from Italian. It should be said that since I'm an ardent Juventus fan my admiration for Michel Platini first and Zinédine Zidane second has reinforced my bond with France. And I have to admit that I've always been very drawn to the Maghrebi. I don't know why. I love their music and their food. Years ago I had a lovely but short romance with a girl of Moroccan origin, who lived in a Paris suburb.

On the funicular, I sit next to two red-haired brothers. From the green sweater of the younger one, with the symbol of a harp, I deduce that they're Irish. The journey is pleasant. There's an invisible and witty guide who rattles off tourist information. For example, Marseilles was founded by Greeks more than two thousand years ago; also, a scene in a famous Marcel Pagnol film was shot in one of the streets in the Vieux-Port. Obviously there's no mention of the other Marseilles, the city of the northern neighborhoods like Busserine, Les Flamants, Castellane, and Bassens, where crime reigns.

The giant toy continues to ascend. Finally we reach the top. Jean-Pierre always jokes that the Marseillais are the poor cousins of the Italians and the Greeks in terms of archeological treasures. They have hardly any monuments. But the Vieux-Port is more beautiful from here. While I sit admiring the view, a phone call arrives from the paper. I heave a sigh, and off I go with the first lie of the day.

"So, Enzo, what news?"

"The information I've picked up is very sensitive, Angelo."

"Don't worry. I'll be discreet. The sources will stay anonymous."

"Look, it's a serious matter. It's an underworld feud between Albanians and Romanians."

"Albanians and Romanians . . . Continue, Enzo, I'm taking notes."

"The Romanian criminals are making a clean sweep, they feel they're the stronger now, and they're ready to take command. They want to control the market in drugs and prostitution. In three months Romania will enter the European Union. They don't want to be associated with the Albanian clans anymore. They want to be the bosses."

"So they're settling scores in the Mafia way. The Romanians are like the Corleonesi—like Liggio, Provenzano, Riina, and Bagarella."

"You could say that," I confirm.

Isn't it a good comparison? I restrain a laugh. What does the Romanian Bernardo Provenzano look like? Will he be good at living as a fugitive for forty-three years? Will he write notes that quote the Bible? And what about the Romanian Totò Riina? Will he be an old-style boss or does he know how to use the Internet and Skype? Finally, can Romania claim someone like our Leoluca Bagarella?

"And the Albanians are like the Palermo family—Stefano Bontate, Totò Inzerillo, Gaetano Badalamenti, and Tommaso Buscetta. Am I wrong, Enzo?"

"No, you're right."

An Albanian Buscetta! Does he wear glasses that cover half his face or will he settle for contact lenses? Does he have a weakness for pretty women or is a faithful and obedient little wife enough? The Albanian Buscetta! Now I burst out laughing.

"Is that all, Enzo?"

"Yes, for now."

"That's great. If there's news call me. No need for you to come to the office today. Thanks, Enzo."

"Thank *you*."

Maybe I don't deserve a thank-you, because I haven't done anything special. But I'll at least accept congratulations for creativity, vast imagination, and especially performance. I was magnificent. Bravo, Enzo! No problem with your conscience? And why should there be? Did I hurt anyone? I don't think so. All right, let's be clear right away: I don't give a damn if the story of the Albanian-Romanian mafia feud is invented. A hoax, as my colleagues say. Must we be reminded of the study that that English university did, of the world of information?

Ninety per cent of the news published every day is false, and five per cent isn't verified; only the rest is real news. Forget it. I want to take advantage of my brief stay in Marseilles. I go back down to the Vieux-Port in the gigantic toy. The ride down is fantastic. I take a little walk in the area around Rue de la Canebière and go into a bookstore. I glance at what's new. A lot of political books. All having to do with the presidential election campaign coming up in the spring of 2007. Two faces monopolize the covers, Ségolène Royal and Nicolas Sarkozy, but obviously there's no shortage of Jean-Marie Le Pen and his damn smile. Last time it was really close. What if Le Pen were in the Élysée Palace instead of Jacques Chirac? When it comes to scenarios like these, it's better to tell your imagination to fuck off.

It's about a ten-minute walk to Jean-Pierre's house in the Panier. I leave the hotel, on the Quai du Port, carrying two gifts and a bunch of roses. I turn onto Rue de la Prison, then I take Montée des Accoules. The Panier is the soul of Marseilles. It's also the city's memory. There are still traces of Piedmontese and Neapolitan immigrants. Jean-Pierre was born here. His grandfather was a socialist and anti-Fascist who fled Turin in the twenties. More than half the Marseillais are of Italian origin. I met Jean-Pierre ten years ago at the Turin book fair. He came to deliver a talk on Marseilles. The fact that he had Italian origins was an immediate bond between us. I'm very drawn to people who have complicated roots, like me. I was born in Turin to parents from Calabria. In Turin, when I was a child, I was called the Calabrese, while in Calabria I was called the Turinese. In other words, from neither here nor there.

Jean-Pierre is an anthropologist, a few years older than I am. He's married to a teacher and has a teenage son with the same name as me. The son of Zizou, the mythical Zidane, a pedigreed Marseillais, is also named Enzo. It seems that this name became famous in Marseilles after the success of the Uruguayan player Enzo Francescoli, who had an Italian background, on the Olympique de Marseilles team. An undisputed champion. As a Juventus fan I say only: too bad he chose to wear the Turin Toro jersey in the early nineties!

Here I am on the Rue du Refuge, where Jean-Pierre lives. The street is narrow but very welcoming. Food smells saturate the air. I spent two weeks here four years ago. Jean-Pierre and I swapped houses for the summer vacation; at the time I had a Bolognese girlfriend, Francesca, whose accent drove me wild. I'd go to the Vieux-Port to buy fresh fish and do the shopping at the market of Noailles. Those were unforgettable days. I've brought Jean-Pierre's son a Juventus T-shirt that has the name of Trezeguet, a player who's the son of Argentine immigrants. For his wife, Sandrine, the roses. With women I always like to be a gentleman.

"*Mon cher ami* Giampiero."

"You're the only person who calls me that. If my father heard you he'd be furious. You know, he hates being reminded of his Italian roots."

"*Vive l'assimilation!* Now he must be pleased that the son of a Hungarian immigrant could become Président de la République."

"Let's talk about it after dinner, not before, please. Politics, as you know, takes away my appetite."

"Like the Italian championship with mine."

"I understand. It's hard to see Juventus in Series B."

"I swore not to go to the stadium this year."

"You have my full sympathy. I imagine that those lovely roses are not for me."

"No."

"Sandrine is at her mother's; she felt ill suddenly. But aren't you supposed to stay 'til Tuesday?"

"Yes, but unfortunately I had to move up my flight because of an emergency at work. Four Albanians have been killed in Turin."

"A feud?"

"Very likely."

"You remember the clans of the Guérini and the Zampas here in Marseilles? The demise of a clan is always violent."

The criminal world is a subject that fascinates both of us. Evil is more fertile than good, as Machiavelli pointed out. Evil is very creative: it always finds original methods of avoiding control and screwing the law. I agree with Jean-Pierre that there exist similarities between the historical bosses of Marseillais crime, alias the Milieu, like Paul Carbone, Francois Spirito, Antoine Guérini, Gaetano Zampa, and Francis le Belge, and the Albanian and Romanian gangsters in Italy. They all started out with prostitution and continued to act as *proxénète*, pimps.

After this chat we sit down at the table. It's a typical Marseilles dinner: *soupe au pistou*, with aioli, and *tarte tatin*, made by Sandrine. Jean-Pierre never moved out of the Panier. His brothers and sisters left years ago. He decided to give his son an Italian name because he wants to be reconciled with his origins. He has often told me stories of children who were ashamed of their Italian surnames. The same thing happened to us southerners in the cities of northern Italy. When I was at school in Turin my Sicilian, Calabrian, and Neapolitan friends were embarrassed to say that their names were Salvatore, Carmelo, or Rosario. Other kids were always making fun of them. Not to mention the Pasquales, Gennaros, et cetera. Poor kids, they had to endure endless teasing. It's hard not to make a comparison today with the children of immigrants who have Arabic or African names . . .

The *soupe au pistou* and the aioli are heavy but edible, and though the garlic is too strong, it's not a problem—I'm not kissing anybody tonight. The *tarte tatin*, on the other hand, is pretty revolting. I prefer not to make comments. Jean-Pierre might report them to his wife; better to maintain good relations with Sandrine. We move to the living room for coffee. I look with admiration, as always, at the wonderful photograph of Jean-Pierre with his friend Jean-Claude Izzo, the great Marseillais writer, who died six years ago. Too bad, I wasn't in time to meet him in person, but luckily we still have the pleasurable company of his novels.

"It's disgusting everywhere, Enzo. The situation here in Marseilles is untenable. The extreme right is becoming the norm, in fact a model that others are following, not only in France but all over Europe."

"The game is rigged. They play on people's insecurities to rake in votes," I confirm.

"Today the scapegoats are the Arabs, the Africans, and the Gypsies. Yesterday it was the Italians. When I hear talk of integration, it makes me crazy. The Italian immigrants in Marseilles, like you southerners in the north of Italy, were Catholic, white, and European, yet in spite of all that they were heavily discriminated against."

"The newest arrivals are always blamed, *cher* Giampiero."

Jean-Pierre talks to me about the new research he's doing in the northern neighborhoods of Marseilles. That part of the city, made up of agglomerates of working-class housing, the famous HLM projects, is inhabited largely by the descendants of North African immigrants. It's been abandoned, unemployment is high, and it's remembered only during election campaigns. The schools are unable to carry out their educational mission, so for children there's only the street and drug dealing. The management of individual neighborhoods is an extremely important matter, we need experienced administrators, but the question is: where do we get them?

"Enzo, I hope Turin won't follow the Marseilles example."

"Unfortunately, there's no lack of alarm signals in certain neighborhoods like the Barriera in Milan and Porta Palazzo."

I get back to the hotel around midnight. It will be hard to sleep without Taina. My breath is disgusting. I go to bed right away, since I have to get up early tomorrow. The flight to Turin awaits me.

Chapter 2
In This Goddam Media Circus

I arrive at the airport in Turin in the late morning. I have a coffee to wake myself up seriously, and turn on my cell phone to see the exact time. I've never worn a watch; it's just a weight on your wrist. I have an aversion to bracelets, necklaces, and rings, especially wedding rings, which are like handcuffs. My amiable crusade against marriage has no reprieve in sight. Thirty calls without an answer. Same number, I know it well. I call right away.

"What have you been getting up to, Enzu'?"

"What did I do, Mamma?"

"First you make trouble, and then you hide. God give me patience!"

"I don't understand, mamma. What is it?"

"What's this business of the Mafia, eh?"

"Mafia?"

"Sooner or later you'll give me a heart attack."

"Mamma, what is it?"

"I read the article in your newspaper this morning. You got yourself mixed up again in some terrible business of criminals. Just what we needed—Albanian and Romanian mafiosi."

"Mamma, why are you upset?"

"Where are you?"

"Turin."

"Enzu'! Don't take me for a fool. You've been away from home for four days. Your car is still parked in the same place, in front of the butcher, you haven't picked up your mail, you haven't answered the house phone, you haven't . . . "

"It's true, Mamma, I'm back in Turin now. I was on a job for the paper in Venice."

"What does Venice have to do with it? Your article talks about Corleone!"

"Don't worry, Mamma."

"You tell me I mustn't worry and then as usual you do things your own way. I don't even know where you are now. God give me patience!"

"I'm in Turin, Mamma. I swear. You can call me at home in half an hour."

It's useless to lie about my movements. My mother knows everything about me. Better to beat a retreat. Try to cut our losses. Denying is pointless; in fact it makes her more upset. What the fuck is this business about Corleone? What did that shit Maritani write? I have to read it right away. Before getting the bus for the Porta Nuova station, I buy a copy of the paper. I'm riveted to the first page: Mafia-style feud between Albanians and Romanians. And under the headline: Enzo Laganà. I'm on the front page of the national edition. I read the first lines quickly.

> Yesterday morning four bodies were found in Turin. All the victims, two women with no criminal record and two men with arrest records, were Albanian. On the basis of early reconstructions of the facts, our newspaper is able to confirm the hypothesis of a feud within the foreign criminal underworld between Albanians and Romanians. Is a Mafia feud under way, like the one between the Palermo clan and the Corleonesi? Continued on p. 3.

Are they serious? What are they thinking, exposing me on the first page? Just doing me a favor, giving a push to my journalistic career? I go to page three. There are statistics on the Albanian and Romanian immigrant communities in Italy. Here we have the usual goddam confusion between criminal immigrants and respectable ones. There's an article devoted to the Second Mafia War, the one at the start of the eighties that led to the victory of the Corleonesi. Naturally there are photos of the historic bosses: Provenzano, Riina, Buscetta, and the others.

I go back to the first page. On the left is an editorial by the editor-in-chief, Salvini, with the headline IN SEARCH OF LOST SECURITY. The asshole is playing Proust now? The first lines are enough for me to see which way the winds are blowing.

> Security is a precious commodity for our country. Citizens pay, with their taxes, to maintain it. Criminal activities involving foreign citizens have increased in recent times. Foreign criminality has become an undeniable reality. Anxious and anguished, we are witnessing an escalation of violence in our cities. Our newspaper documents this day by day. Now our reporter Enzo Laganà informs us that a feud between Albanian and Romanian criminals is under way, on Italian soil, in our beautiful Turin, the first capital of Italy after Unification, the city of the economic miracle.

Why does he quote me, the son of a bitch? I know him well; he doesn't make a move without calculating every detail. He even weighs his commas. He starts writing his fucking editorials in the morning, and revises them hundreds of times before they go to press. He's always afraid of sticking his neck out. Is he using me as a shield to rebuff possible criticisms? Very likely. He's been criticized often by the shareholders, ever since he assumed editorship of the paper, four years ago. They accuse him of not doing enough to attract advertising and increase sales. In order to do this he aspires to be more like the tabloids, with the objective of selling more copies in order to win a big slice of the advertising pie. In the meantime, he holds himself ready to make the big jump. But where does he want to jump to? Maybe the editorship of a bigger newspaper? Or he wants to get into politics and be a deputy? No one knows, or maybe only he knows. But I don't give a goddam about this. I only want to know why they've slammed me onto the first page twice? Now I know why my mother was so worried. She was right. The phone rings. It's that shit Maritani.

"Have you seen our scoop, Enzo?"

"Yes, I've read the paper."

"We were the only ones who had the story about the feud between the Albanians and the Romanians."

"Bravo."

"We beat the competition. Happy about the first page?"

"Very happy. It's all thanks to you. You're the one who wrote the article."

"I just organized your information. You're the one who discovered our Deep Throat. By the way, the editor-in-chief called me. He wanted to know who our source is on the feud."

"The source is secret."

"I told him that, but he was very insistent."

"I can't expose my sources, Angelo. It's a professional secret."

"Of course, but I would remind you that the editor of the Washington *Post*, Ben Bradlee, also knew Bob Woodward and Carl Bernstein's secret. So our editor has the right, in fact the duty, to know."

"I promised to keep it a secret, Angelo."

Now I understand why I had the honor of the first page. No one wants to take the risk. If I remember correctly, in the film *All the President's Men* it's only Woodward, alias Redford, who knows the identity of Deep Throat. Apparently, now there is a new and very original version of the facts, compliments of Angelo Maritani, the editor of the local edition of an Italian daily.

When I get home I make some noise to let spy No. 1 know I'm back. I open the window and go out on the small balcony. I barely have time to turn around before I hear her voice.

"Here you are, you're back. Did you talk to your mother?"

"Yes, auntie."

"She was looking for you this morning. You mustn't cause her to worry like that! Poor woman!"

"There's nothing to worry about."

"Little children little trouble, big children big trouble."

"What pearls of wisdom, auntie!"

This proverb really pisses me off. I don't know exactly if it's Sicilian or Calabrian. Certainly it's southern. Everyone complains about their children. I wonder, and not just to be argumentative: if children are such a pain in the ass, why have them? Aunt Giovanna alias Quiz (she is mad about television quiz shows), isn't a real aunt but a friend of my mother's. She turned eighty a few months ago and is in really good health. She's been a widow for ten years, living by herself since her daughter emigrated to Canada. She talks to my mother every day for hours and hours—they started it when intercity phone calls became free. Obviously, they devote almost all their time to yours truly.

"Enzo, all hell has broken loose in your absence."

"The feud between the Albanians and the Romanians?"

"No, I mean here in the neighborhood."

"What happened?"

"The Muslims of the mosque on Via Galliari have sworn to tear the Nigerian on the third floor to pieces."

"Joseph? What did he do?"

"His piglet did something very stupid."

"Piglet?"

Aunt Quiz has a gift for directness, she gets to the point without a lot of beating around the bush. Which is really lucky for someone like me—I can't stand long preliminaries. I hear the story of Joseph's piglet. Two nights ago, someone (perhaps more than one person) sneaked a piglet into the local mosque, then made a video of the pig walking calmly and happily around the prayer room. For the mosque-goers it's the ultimate provocation, after a lot of pressure to close the place—originally a dressmaker's. I remember that the opening of the small mosque, four years ago, was controversial, and greeted by protests from some of the residents of San Salvario. The business encouraged a group of them to form a committee called Masters in Our Own House. Among its goals: to close the mosque on Via Galliari and prevent the opening of others, pressure the city to withdraw licenses from halal butchers, kebab shops, and on and on. The list is very long. The phone rings.

"Really, Enzu', pull yourself together. God give me patience! You're not a child. You're thirty-seven years old. At your age I already had two children, a girl sixteen and a disastrous son of eighteen, that is you."

"Come on, Mamma."

"Your sister has been settled for years, with a fine husband and beautiful children, living happily in Detroit, while you . . . "

"What am I supposed to do? You can't fit a square peg in a round hole."

"Talking to you is no use. Anyway I'm not going to get angry anymore. Listen, remember to eat the turkey in the fridge today or tomorrow, because it expires the ninth of October. And the eggs the twelfth of October."

"All right."

"Don't forget to pay the gas bill, it's due the sixteenth."

"Yes, ma'am!"

My mother even knows what's in the refrigerator. Let's clear up a possible mistake: she's not a witch or a seer. She's just a very well-informed woman. That's all. Credit goes to Natalia, who comes to clean every Wednesday. After work she reports everything. Natalia is spy No. 2. My mother lives in Calabria, in Cosenza, but she knows everything I do here in Turin: what I eat, who I'm with, how I'm dressed, what time I get home at night. My habitat is frequented by two women who spy for her. Aunt Giovanna, alias Quiz, lives next door; her apartment shares a wall with mine. She is really good, she notices everything. She even knows what time I go to bed, when I get up, and maybe how many times I go to the bathroom. She has an ear that never betrays her. I've always said that she's a wasted resource, she'd be a perfect spy disguised as a housewife. She observes all my movements. She demonstrates her spying skills and gifts in particular when I bring a woman home. She goes on general alert, and presents a detailed report to her boss with a lot of useful information for putting together the visitor's identikit: is she a brunette, black-haired, or a blonde? How old is she? Is she fat or thin? Tall or short? How is she dressed? What perfume is she wearing? . . . It should absolutely not be forgotten that this is all thanks to my mother, who has set up a real spy agency. I am the only target. My friend Sam calls it a "safety net," consistent with the phenomenon of the Mediterranean mamma, the famous Big Mama. How much do these spying operations cost? How does my mother pay her spies? In this battle she arrays all her weapons with assurance: Calabrian sweets and other goodies. Whenever she comes to Turin, she brings generous rewards for her two employees. Over time, my mother's pressure on me has increased. To her I'm a puzzle because I'm not married and I don't have children. I'm a bachelor, a *schetto* to marry off at all costs. I, on the other hand, see myself as a wonderful single man. Anyway, she's told me clearly many times, "I'll leave you in peace when you have a wife. For me you're still a child to take care of." Marvelous, a child of thirty-seven!

My mother has always talked to me a bit in Calabrian; she refused to follow the recommendations of the teachers on the importance of using exclusively Italian with one's children. Once, after the hundredth warning, she answered, in dialect, "At my house *parru cumu me piacia* . . . I speak however I want." My father always used to say that human beings have the same fate as trees: deprived of their roots, they die. And there is no stronger root than language. I think he was right. A person who leaves his own land is like a tree that's transplanted somewhere else: it can be fatal to deprive it of its roots.

In the afternoon I watch the soccer games on Sky. It's always torture. Who would have thought? Juventus in Series B! We poor Juventus fans. We have to endure teasing from everyone, especially Toro fans. Should the truth be told or not? So let's say it: the Italian Championship has no flavor, in fact it's revolting. A championship without Juve is like the World Cup without Brazil. Before, I couldn't stand Toro: you can't be born and grow up in Turin without taking sides in soccer. Now I hate them all: Milan, Inter, Rome, Lazio . . .

Today the fucking anti-Juventus shits have reared their heads. They don't miss a chance to attack Juventus. Before the scandal, they did it indirectly with stadium chants, now they do it openly, without embarrassment. They claim that we corrupted the referees with Fiat money in order to win trophies and cups. Bullshit. Envy is a terrible sickness and has no cure. I'm tempted to console myself by watching some Juve games from the days of Platini or Zidane. I have an excellent DVD collection, but I hate nostalgia and people who are nostalgic. I settle the matter by turning off the TV. I put on a CD of my favorite singer. The voice of Rino Gaetano always boosts my morale.

> Ever since you went away, ever since you've been gone
> Ever since the pasta's burned I don't eat it anymore
> Ah, Maria, you're the one I miss . . .

Afterward, not having a damn thing to do, I decide to stop in at the newspaper office, which is on Via Garibaldi. This gives me an opportunity for a good walk. It takes twenty minutes on foot from my house. It's important to show up after the scoop. I, too, have the right to my fifteen minutes of fame. I've barely sat down at my desk when I see Maritani coming, with a big smile, waving a sheet of paper.

"Enzo, a very important news bulletin, it just arrived a few minutes ago. I'll read it to you: 'Turin, 4:35 P.M. The agents of the San Donato police station have discovered three dead bodies in the Barrera area of Milan. The victims have been identified, they are of Romanian nationality. There are two young men: Stefan Steriscu, thirty, Florin Georgescu, twenty-five, and a woman, Larisa Ropotan, twenty-three. The bodies suffered genital mutilation, like the murdered Albanians discovered in Turin yesterday morning. Today's edition of a national daily brought the news that a feud is under way between Albanian and Romanian criminals.' We've hit the jackpot. Really, congratulations!"

"Thank you."

"The editor-in-chief called me again from the main office, he insists on knowing the identity of the source. I'm afraid it's no longer possible to hide it."

I have no other choice. In this fucking media circus you have to play to the end. Let's invent a source!

"So who is our source?"

"An Albanian criminal."

"So he belongs to the side that's fallen into disgrace, a sort of Buscetta."

"Yes, you could say that," I affirm.

What can I do? The delusion is unstoppable!

"O.K., an Albanian Buscetta. But there's a substantial difference. Tommaso Buscetta confessed to a judge, Giovanni Falcone. The Albanian Buscetta instead will speak to a journalist, Enzo Laganà."

"How times change!"

I'm no longer paying attention to his observations. Maritani is the typical Milanese who is always trying to show off his Lombard origins, the first-in-the-class syndrome. His accent really irritates me. He often becomes ponderous, and insufferable. He sums up the situation repeating stuff I've heard him say on many occasions, and that is that in life you always have to take chances, for example play an attacking game, like Sacchi's Milan team; that the stakes are high, and you have to respond to challenges. And also that in the media world the chain defense, that odious defensive game, doesn't work. And that you mustn't back down by a millimeter, rather, you have to surprise, as we've done so far. After some circling around and a warmup phase he arrives at the point.

"You have to persuade our Deep Throat to come out."

"Come out? In what sense?"

"Give us an interview."

"It's impossible."

I point out some difficulties. For example, if the source doesn't want to expose himself anymore, what can I do? I can't force him. Maritani insists: don't force but persuade. If our Deep Throat wants to play the Albanian Buscetta he has to talk, like the boss Tommaso Buscetta. The public has the sacrosanct right to know what is happening.

Maritani explains the strategy we're going to follow. First of all we have to play the card of our secret source well. A lot of people are envious of our success, unfair competitors and nasty jackals of all types who spread falsehoods about our newspaper. There are even some who claim that we have no source, that is, that we invented everything out of whole cloth. What sort of disgusting world do we work in? But for that very reason we have to persuade the Albanian Buscetta to go public, give us an interview. I remind Maritani that yesterday's pact about the source was not this, but he answers that situations evolve and one has to adapt to them. There is pressure from the main office. We have no choice.

I know Maritani, he won't let go. Now, however, I have a serious problem to solve and not much time. I have to give life to a phantom, give him a name that might be "the Albanian Buscetta." Or at least give him a voice. A wicked idea starts buzzing in my head. Later, to put it into practice, I call my friend Luciano Terni and we agree to meet at his house at Porta Palazzo around ten.

Luciano Terni is a good friend; we've known each other since high school. He's tall and thin, and has an extraordinary gift: he can imitate any voice. He's a great actor and he also does a lot of volunteering. He works with poor kids, mostly immigrants, using theater. He knows the immigrant world really well. I go to him for "artistic odd jobs." He's my secret weapon against the bureaucracy. As my mother always says, I wasn't blessed with patience. To get papers released, or access to a classified document, you need applications, permissions, infinite authorizations. However, telephone calls from high places are also sufficient, with the usual phrase: "Make available to Mr. Enzo Laganà whatever he wants." The trick is very simple: I ask the good Luciano to make a phone call in which he imitates the voice of the person in charge. First, I give him a recording of the voice, obtained illegally. And being a perfectionist he does his best. The result has always been excellent. Since the job is sensitive and risky we've adopted some measures used by the Services. Never speak to each other on the "official" telephone during the imitations, in order not to be intercepted. The most secure method is to use the cell phone of a ghost, that is, registered to a deceased person. We've never had problems. And we often have a lot of fun cheating some assholes.

I have to admit that I was very much inspired by Alighiero

Noschese in perfecting my Luciano. Noschese was an extraordinary imitator; he did marvelous imitations of famous characters like Giulio Andreotti. In 1979 he was found dead, a suicide, in mysterious circumstances at the Villa Stuart clinic in Rome, where he had been admitted for serious depression. The official version said he had shot himself with a pistol. Two years later the list of those who were enrolled in P2 came out, and among them was the name of the great Alighiero. But what was someone like Noschese doing with the powerful of the moment? Maybe the answer is contained in an interview with an anonymous general that appeared in *Espresso* in 1981: during the Years of Lead, a great imitator was used to derail investigations into the bombings by means of a series of phone calls attributed to important institutional figures.

"Congratulations on the front page, Enzo."

"Thanks. Unfortunately there's some collateral damage."

"What have you done this time?"

"Nothing irreparable, Luciano."

"That means you're in trouble and you need my help."

"I'd say that's right. But first I have to confess something. In the story it says there's a feud."

"Between Albanians and Romanians."

"Yes. I made it up, in order to screw those shits at the paper."

"And if they find out that you invented the whole thing?"

"There would be quite a scandal."

"You'll finally get your chance to change careers."

"Right. But now I need you to complete the job. We have to give a voice to the ghost, my secret source."

"Then give me the script."

I give Luciano instructions, along with tips and suggestions for interpreting the character. I feel like a great director who leaves the actors a lot of freedom to improvise. So our character should be a cross between an Albanian criminal who lives in Italy and Tommaso Buscetta. He's between forty and fifty. He's a powerful man, but has been discredited. He fears for his life after the murder of his associates. He's encircled, like a gravely wounded lion, and is desperately seeking a way out. He doesn't trust anyone. He should talk a little bit about his childhood. It wouldn't hurt to get some inspiration from the first part of Sergio Leone's *Once Upon a Time in America*. He should recount the various stages of his criminal career. References to *Godfather I, II*, and *III* also wouldn't hurt, and to the character of Scarface, played by my idol, Al Pacino. Then there is an important point to develop that concerns relations with the Romanians. First, they were simply collaborators associated with the Albanians, then they got swelled heads, and now they want to work for themselves.

I alert him to Maritani's questions. We agree on a compensation of three thousand euros, to be given to charity, and on the schedule for the interview: tomorrow at three in the afternoon. The operation is risky, but I don't care. If I'm discovered I'll be thrown off the newspaper and probably barred from carrying a press card again. So I'll finally cut the damn umbilical cord. I started as a reporter at twenty, before graduating with a degree in sociology. I had clear ideas about what I wanted and a dream to fulfill: to be an investigative reporter. Over the many years since then I've accumulated frustrations and disappointments. Sooner or later I'll have to confront the situation and end my relationship with this profession.

Chapter 3
Do You Grow Basil in the Bathtub?

Italy is a country of connections. There's no room for merit. Proof? Aunt Giovanna, born in 1926, is living proof. She began applying to participate on television quiz shows at the time of *Leave It or Double It*. No one has ever called her. Isn't that shameful? Every year she swears she won't pay her RAI charge, then at the last minute she backs off. You can't change the habits of a lifetime.

My aunt is very disappointed: it's a real pity that she won't be able to transmit her knowledge to future generations. Over the decades she has developed great expertise in quizzes. Often she reveals certain secrets of winning: concentrate hard, listen to the m.c. carefully, never underestimate simple questions, which can have hidden traps, don't pay attention to the audience applause, don't be distracted by the cameras. I listen to my aunt's usual complaints as I go down the stairs.

I stop at the café for breakfast, cappuccino and whole-wheat honey croissant. Giacomo, the owner, is around fifty. He inherited the café from his father. Although he has all the virtues in the world, he has one very serious defect: he's a Toro fan. Luckily he's not a pain in the ass, extremist, contentious, combative. In other words, he knows how to put up with and manage his Juventus envy with elegance and diplomacy, because he doesn't want to lose customers. That suits me fine. To console himself and endure the continuous frustrations provoked by his favorite team, Giacomo has a collection of photos of the famous match against Juventus in 1983 won by the Toro, 3–2. A real joke, because Juve won, 2–0. The photos are everywhere in the café, even in the bathroom.

As soon as I sit down, I see Mario Bellezza arriving. He smiles and sits down next to me. I wonder: why can't I enjoy my breakfast in blessed peace? Bellezza is around seventy, and could never go unnoticed: he has the biggest belly in San Salvario. And a weakness for beer. He is a true connoisseur. Ever since he retired he's been of the opinion that he's the neighborhood leader. He's like the rooster in the henhouse. He's constantly forming committees in defense of something or other. He never gets tired of it. Lately he's taken it into his head to set up neighborhood watch patrols. What will become of the cops and the carabinieri? Will they be fired? Take early retirement? His great project, however, is to organize a referendum in San Salvario on the closing of all the mosques and prayer rooms. Obviously, only Italians will be able to vote. I think he makes all this fuss in order not to get bored. For years he worked with my father at Fiat. Which explains those somewhat paternal attitudes of his that make me furious.

"Congratulations, Enzo. Your father would be very proud of you."

"Thanks."

"Those non-E.U. bastards act like masters in our house. We can't put up with it any longer. It's time to send them off with a kick in the ass."

"May I buy you a coffee?"

"Coffee? Your scoop on the new mafia war deserves a celebration."

"How about a beer?"

"We'll have another chance, but now we have to get busy. Listen, Enzo, I'd like to ask your help."

"Yes?"

"Could you publish our petition in your paper?"

"What's it about?"

"An appeal to save that poor Gino."

"Gino? Who's that?"

"The piglet that those shit Muslims want to kill."

"Really?"

So Joseph's pig has a name. Maybe he has a surname, too. Bellezza gives me a general picture of the situation. One fact is important above all. The piglet in question is a pure Piedmontese. He wasn't imported from anywhere. He's not made in China, so to speak. We import everything from China these days, even the tomatoes we use for pasta and pizza. Bellezza is very insistent on the fact that Gino isn't a foreigner or an immigrant but, rather, a native, a true child of the country, in other words like American Indians or Australian aborigines. He therefore deserves to be protected. I have to admit my ignorance. I didn't know there was a Piedmontese breed of pig. I only know about Sardinian sheep, or Carrù oxen, the prized meat from Piedmont. Bellezza has very clear ideas. The call to save Gino the piglet is aimed above all at making the residents of San Salvario aware of the neighborhood's deterioration. It goes without saying that the immigrants, especially the ones from Muslim countries, are the obvious cause of it. The gravest danger is the mosques, like the one on Via Galliari—real time bombs, places outside any controls. To be more convincing, Bellezza takes out of his briefcase a file full of newspaper clippings, and asks me to glance at a couple of articles. I realize from the headlines that they have to do with the attacks of September 11, 2001. It crosses my mind to ask him: what the hell do these have to do with the piglet? Bellezza explains to me that the attacks on the Twin Towers were planned in a small mosque in Hamburg, just like the one on Via Galliari. If there is a valuable lesson to be drawn, surely it is never to underestimate the Muslim threat.

"Enzo, the business of the piglet is only a pretense."

"In what sense?"

Here we arrive punctually at the conspiracy theory. The Muslims of the mosque have invented the whole thing out of nothing to test our strength. They feel powerful enough, like the goddam Albanian and Romanian mafiosi, to impose their rules in our house. They have chosen poor Gino as a means of flexing their muscles. It's all there. Will they stop at that? Absolutely not. Today they don't want Gino near their damn mosque, tomorrow they'll move on to something else. They'll say they don't want pork in the neighborhood butcher shops or restaurants or in the Madama Cristina market. Will it stop there? No. Sooner or later it will be the women's turn. They'll say that girls can't wear miniskirts and shorts. All right, sure, let's pretend we live in the Middle Ages. Do you want anything else? Nothing much, we just want women to wear the burkha. One little step at a time. That's how it happened with the Taliban in Afghanistan. Will it end there? No. They'll do all they can to ban alcohol, including beer. When Bellezza evokes beer, his eyes light up. His gaze becomes threatening. He's like an animal ready to attack to defend its young.

"God damn! I can't even imagine life without a mug of cold beer. It would be like roasted peppers without the *bagnacauda*. Let them go home."

"Taking a pig to a mosque is extremely offensive."

"Enzo, I repeat, the pig is only a pretext. At stake is our dignity and our honor, I would say the defense of our identity."

"What does a pig have to do with our identity?"

There are things that escape me. I admit I can't grasp certain concepts on my own. Luckily there are people who are enlightened and blessed with wisdom, like Mario Bellezza, who launches into his argument again. Muslims, unlike us, don't eat pork because it's *haram*, not allowed. Thus an insurmountable barrier is set up between us and them. A Piedmontese pig like Gino, who is Italian, or, rather, *very* Italian, becomes a symbol, a flag, a bulwark to safeguard our

Italianness. And since my mind is not creative, especially in the morning, Bellezza takes advantage of this and drags me into a long, very intellectual monologue on the integration of foreigners into our country.

"For me, integration means accepting everything," he declares.

"That's not integration but assimilation, colonialism."

"I don't give a goddam. If a Muslim immigrant comes and tells me he wants to stay in our country and maybe become an Italian citizen, you know what I ask him?"

"What?"

"Do you like beer? Do you eat prosciutto?"

"And if he says no?"

"Dear Muslim, I'm sorry, but you don't have the necessary qualifications."

"Very interesting."

So we should add to the qualifications for citizenship the pork test. Maybe it will be more decisive than the Italian language test. Look, if there's a word that pisses me off it's certainly that one: integration! I've heard it ever since I was born. People like Bellezza don't remember or maybe don't want to remember the ugly welcome that southerners got in northern cities like Milan and Turin. They arrived at Porta Nuova after a long journey on the *treno del sole*, the sun train, which, starting from Palermo and Siracusa, formed a single convoy, and traveled through Calabria, Basilicata, Campania, Lazio, Tuscany, and Liguria. Then, too, as now, it was said that the new arrivals (called *napuli* or even Moroccans) could not be "integrated." They were painted as backward, illiterate, dangerous—carriers of crime of every sort. Much better to keep them at a distance. "We don't rent to southerners" was the slogan of that welcome, soon forgotten. I remember, I remember it all: the laughter of my classmates when my last name was pronounced: Laganà! Yes, I was ashamed and wished for a different name, not a Calabrian name, but one as northern as possible. I remember the questions they asked when I was a child: "Is it true that you grow basil in the bathtub?" and "Why are you lazy good-for-nothings?" Such scorn, such humiliation. Then people thought it was better to hide the shit under the carpet. Turn the page without even reading it. I wonder: could there possibly be integration without acceptance, without respect, without understanding, without memory?

I use this encounter with Bellezza to clarify things a little. I ask him directly if his committee is involved in *l'affaire* Gino, but he denies it. Recently a political party legitimately represented in the Italian parliament organized a Pig Day, a campaign against mosques. It wouldn't be that surprising if this fashion had reached even San Salvario. Fashions, like globalization, know no boundaries.

Returning to the petition to save Gino the piglet, I tell Bellezza that I can't promise that his petition will be published (the truth is that it will be thrown into the wastebasket immediately). I am simply a reporter, it's the editor who has to decide. He thanks me warmly.

"Enzo, remember that with the Muslims we must never lower our guard. You know why?"

"Why."

"Because they'll stick it up our ass. Is that clear?"

"Very clear."

I arrive at the paper at lunchtime and go directly to Maritani's office. My plan is ready for execution. I take a deep breath, knock, and enter. I tell him without wasting time that the Albanian Buscetta has agreed to be interviewed by phone.

"We can't meet Deep Throat in person, Enzo?"

"Unfortunately it can't be done."

I expected this question. By now Maritani has fully identified with the journalist Woodward. He wants to meet Deep Throat in person, maybe in an isolated place in the middle of the night. I try to justify the choice of the telephone. The Albanian Buscetta is hiding in Turin in a secret place. He's afraid of being killed. He doesn't trust anyone. It's very dangerous to meet him, he's a parcel bomb, a loose cannon, better to keep our distance. Anyone who comes close to him would be risking his own life. Maritani can't hide his disappointment. What can we do? In life you have to be satisfied. Then I move on to the logistical aspects of the interview. We need a safe place outside the newspaper. In the office there's the danger of being tapped. Maritani proposes his sister's apartment, near the Olympic stadium. She's in Argentina and no one's living there. To create some suspense and increase the adrenaline, I tell him that there is a strong likelihood that someone is watching us. So we should take every precaution: leave separately, use public transportation in order not to be followed, and other nonsense.

As for the three thousand euros, the compensation for the interview, Maritani doesn't make trouble. Exclusive interviews are not free. My performance is very convincing. I decide to go and eat before hearing, at last, the voice of the Albanian Buscetta.

Here are the two of us, waiting for Hour X. We sit in the kitchen. The window is closed. There's not much light. Poor Maritani is a lot more excited than I am. He's living a magical moment. He's watching again in his mind the scene in *All the President's Men* where, at two in the morning, in an underground parking garage, Redford alias Woodward meets Felt alias Deep Throat. A spine-chilling scene. Soon we'll hear the mysterious voice. I put my cell phone with the ghost number on the table. Maritani takes a small digital tape recorder out of his pocket. Here's the call from Luciano alias the Albanian

Buscetta. I press the green button and activate the speaker phone.

"Hello, it's me."

"Laganà speaking. As agreed I'm here with my editor, Maritani."

"*Mir*, good."

"Hello, I'm Maritani, the editor. First of all I'd like to thank you for agreeing to this interview."

"No interview without money."

"No problem. We've taken care of that. Laganà will deliver the three thousand euros to you."

"What? Three thousand euros? *Rochka*, shit! You take me for a *kurve*, a starving prostitute?"

This was not in the script! Improvisation No. 1.

"I'm sorry, didn't you ask for three thousand euros?"

"Yes, but that was yesterday. I'm a fan of the market, stocks up and stocks down. Today my stock has doubled."

"Six thousand euros! Isn't that a little much?"

"I don't give a *rochka!* That's the figure or I'll look for other newspapers. I need that money. I'm hunted, they want to kill me like a dog. I have to get far away from Italy. I have to change my face. I need operations on my nose, my lips."

"All right, we'll give you double. Listen, our readers will want to know everything about you. Your personal and professional story. What would you like us to call you, if you don't want to say your real name?"

"Call me Luan; in my language it means lion. I am and remain the boss of all!"

The performance of Luciano, alias the Albanian Buscetta, is magnificent. The accent is perfect. He has prepared the part perfectly. He's gone beyond the script with masterly improvisation.

When we get back to the office, Maritani gives me two jobs. First: prepare a brief profile of Tommaso Buscetta. Maybe the new generations don't know him, and so I do a rapid search on the Internet to gather information. Second: transcribe the interview in the form of a first-person narrative. He tells me to eliminate the swear words, repeating the famous remark of Ben Bradlee, the editor of the Washington *Post:* "This is a family newspaper." It doesn't take long to put together the story of the Albanian Buscetta. Maritani makes a few corrections, then calls the editor, Salvini, who, after listening to the piece read, authorizes its publication. The editor congratulates me and I thank him. Maritani seems happy and satisfied, he gives me an envelope with the six thousand euros. Obviously it's all under the table, no receipts. A good sum for charity. How many African babies will be adopted long-distance in the next few days?

That night I decide to go to Biberon, a nice bar on Via Silvio Pellico, which opened almost two years ago and is run by two friends, Paola and Sergio. You can taste various types of rum from all over the world and hear good music. Until fairly recently San Salvario was overrun with drug dealers, but now the situation is improving. At Biberon my friend Sam is performing. I arrive a little late and can't find a place to sit. The guy is becoming a star. It's time to get busy and find him a manager. He's really good. I order a beer and lean against the wall. On my left I see a girl in raptures, she must be a student. Sam doesn't miss a chance, he's a first-rate hunter. And in fact now he's noticed her, and he won't let her out of his sight. So begins a long visual courtship.

I met Sam, diminutive of Samir, in 1998. He had just arrived in Turin from Tangiers. After he'd been here illegally for four years, I hired him as a housecleaner so he could get a residency permit, but he paid the social security himself. As soon as he got the permit, he asked me to fire him. It's the only time in my life I've hired a worker and then fired him. Being a boss is not for me. Anyway, officially he's a domestic worker, as it says on his residence permit, but unofficially he's an artist. In music he's a real genius, he can play any instrument he picks up.

Sam's story is no different from that of millions of North African youths who have just one idea in their heads: to get away, at all costs. It's a story I know too well, having heard it directly from him many times. Sam really likes to repeat this North African proverb: "You can't cross a river without getting wet." To achieve a goal or realize a dream you always have to pay a price. Life doesn't give you anything. This my Moroccan friend had reckoned with before he started his adventure as a *harraga*. It's an Algerian term that literally means "to burn" the sea, and it's used to describe a dangerous crossing in a ramshackle boat. Very often it's an extreme journey, one-way only, because of the risk of drowning. The word "burn" probably refers to documents: traveling without a passport, without a visa, and without a ticket.

Sam began dreaming of Europe as a child, because it was very close to his native city, in northern Morocco. It took only a few minutes to cross the Straits of Gibraltar; in fact the distance that separates Africa from Europe is just a few kilometers. To be precise: only fourteen fucking kilometers.

He dreamed a lot as a child; he believed that on the other side there were only blond, blue-eyed children with straight hair. Their parents showered them with gifts, with chocolate and candy every day, because they were very rich, unlike his parents, who always had trouble making it to the end of the month.

In childhood he developed a strong feeling of injustice. He said to himself, "My God! Why didn't you bring me into the world fourteen kilometers to the north? What did I do wrong?" He was always told it's a matter of *maktùb*, destiny: everything is decided before you're born, so you should always be satisfied. God has his blessed reasons and never makes a mistake.

The situation got worse during and after adolescence. He

continued to think obsessively about his European contemporaries, free to kiss girls in public without fear and to demonstrate in the streets without being arrested and tortured.

Eight years ago he decided to change his destiny. He was twenty-five, a graduate of the conservatory, and had a dream to fulfill: to become a great musician. To reach the European El Dorado he made two crossings. First he had to secretly cross the Algerian and Libyan desert, then he paid for a place on a run-down boat loaded with desperate Somalis, Senegalese, Nigerians, North Africans, Palestinians, Kurds, Pakistanis, and others.

It's very hard to describe that experience: suffice to say that he looked death in the face. He prayed a lot, even though he's not in the least observant, begging God insistently to forgive him for not obeying his will: He wished him to be born in Morocco, to live and die there, but Sam rebelled.

They nearly drowned, but were rescued by an Italian military ship. Divine mercy is immense. After a few days in a detention center for illegals in Sicily, he was released, with an expulsion order that gave him two weeks to leave Italian territory.

He tore up the piece of paper the same day, because he had no intention of returning to Morocco. He had just arrived in Italy, in Europe, in paradise, after so many sacrifices. In other words, now that he had reached paradise, he deserved to stay there forever.

So he followed the advice of a young Tunisian who told him to go to Naples, because there was a lot of work in the surrounding areas. The tomato harvest had just begun. He got there in a couple of days, but in place of "a lot of work" he found "a lot of despair": hundreds of young Africans, Asians, and Eastern Europeans, packed like mice into shantytowns, reduced to slavery in the fields and controlled by ruthless overseers. There was misery everywhere; even the Italians were suffering, between unemployment and the Camorra.

He endured that inferno for a week, then he decided to keep going north, to Turin, the city of Fiat and Juventus.

Sam takes a break and comes over to see me. In the meantime a table has opened up. We sit down.

"Thanks for playing that piece I'm so fond of."

"You know I like to make people happy."

"Especially pretty girls."

"Why don't you mind your own business."

"Is that how you speak to your boss?"

"Ex-boss, luckily."

"You'd better be respectful, once a boss always a boss."

"Fuck off, boss! Let's talk about more serious things. What's this story of the feud?"

"All smoke."

"I don't understand."

Sam is a friend I can trust. I summarize the story, beginning with Marseilles, and the famous phone call from Maritani, up to the creation of the character of the Albanian Buscetta. Obviously I don't reveal the identity of Luciano Terni. That is my state secret.

"You're crazy, Enzo."

"Better to be crazy than a jerk."

After the "alleged" feud between Romanians and Albanians, we move on to Joseph's piglet.

"Tell me this thing is just a joke."

"No, it's really serious, Enzo. Joseph ought to get out of sight right away."

"Come on! Joseph is a good guy. He would never do something idiotic like that," I insist.

"The pig that took a walk in the mosque is his."

"Maybe someone wants to frame him."

"A plot against Joseph! Don't talk nonsense. He needs treatment. Someone who mistakes a pig for a cat or a dog is not a normal person—I would say he's sort of a halfwit."

"Now you're acting the racist psychologist," I say, attacking him.

"You know you're absolutely the first person ever to call me a racist?"

"And I certainly won't be the last if you keep talking nonsense like that."

Sam urges me again and again to persuade Joseph to go into hiding outside of Turin for a while, until things settle down. A confrontation is under way. The Muslims of the mosque have to react, and quickly, to defend their credibility. They don't want to lose face. It's easy to say that Joseph is nuts, but the reality is more complex. Joseph has his vision of the world, his logic, his truth. That's it. And who possesses the perfect, absolute, unshakable truth?

Finally Sam says goodbye and joins his new prey, the enraptured student. I, instead, go home with a single desire: sleep.

Chapter 4
Where the Mud Is Sweeter Than Honey

My name is Luan, and I'm forty years old. I was born in Albania, in Durrës, which in my language is pronounced *Dùrs*. It's the most important city after Tirana, the capital, with a population of two hundred and twenty thousand. The sea is beautiful there. How I miss my city! As our proverb goes, *Ku eshte balta me e embel se mjalta*, where the mud is sweeter than honey. I have a very large family, six brothers and five sisters. I'm number ten, like Diego Armando Maradona. Mamma died many years ago, and now she's in Paradise, because she was a good woman. Papa is dead, too, but he's in Hell, because he was a shit. He loved wine and he loved to beat his wife and children. I went to school, but only for three years. I was smart, first in the class. Papa said that school is useless. He decided to send me to work in the fields with my older brothers.

One day Papa hit me and I socked him back. He threw me out of the house. I began to steal, everything from hens to sheep, from bicycles to cars. I was very good at stealing from houses—my great specialty. I belonged to a gang that made a lot of money, but in lekë. Albanian money is wastepaper. Today ten thousand lekë isn't even worth seventy-five euros. We wanted to make real money: marks, francs, pounds, dollars, lire, pesetas . . .

I'm married, and I have two wives. The first is Albanian and lives in Albania; the second is Italian. I'm a Muslim, I can have four wives, not like you poor Christians, forced to marry an official wife and then keep a lot of secret wives, your lovers. The Church says: a single wife for your whole life and no divorce. That I don't like. Men have many needs. They should have many women. It's natural. For me, two wives aren't enough. I have many girls at my disposal, of all races: white, black, European, African, Chinese. I have six children, but I won't tell you where they are. They could be killed, too. I miss them, especially the youngest.

I speak Albanian, German, French, Italian, a little Spanish, and a little English. I can curse in Romanian, Serbian, Polish, Russian, Chinese, Nigerian, Arabic, Moldavian, Hindu, Portuguese, Turkish, and Japanese. And I know how to say "fuck off" in almost all the languages of the world. In our work you need to know languages and, in particular, curses.

In 1992 my best friend Ron and I went to Germany and asked for political asylum as Kosovars. We told a pack of lies—for example that we were tortured by Milosevich's police. The Germans believed us. After two months they gave us papers, a house, and a job. But we had no desire to work five days a week, six hours a day. We weren't used to it. We were only good at stealing. Unfortunately the situation was very difficult. We weren't able to integrate ourselves into Germany. There's no integration for people like us. The cops are on the spot like German shepherds. The laws are shit. For a small supermarket theft you get two years in jail. It's not right. It's too much. After a robbery in a jewelry store my friend was arrested. So I fled to France. But I didn't like it there, either, because the French police are like Dobermans. The judges are shits, they sentence you without mercy. Paris is beautiful, but France was not a country for me. I couldn't fit in there, either.

In 1995 I came to Italy, because I had a cousin here. I got documents under the Dini government amnesty. We set up a gang for dealing drugs, then we invested a lot of money in prostitution. We took girls from Albania and Eastern Europe.

A great business. For me Italy was a paradise. I felt integrated immediately. Unfortunately now it's becoming a real inferno!

The Romanians are bastards. We Albanian bosses gave them bread when they were dying of hunger. First they kissed our hand, now they want to bite it. We've always respected the Romanians. We've always been very generous. We never favored our Albanian girls over their Romanians. For us, all whores are the same. Our Romanian associates always got their money. We were their teachers, from us they learned the secrets of the trade: dealing drugs and exploiting the girls. It's a big market. There's room for everyone. Why kill us like dogs? The business requires tranquility and stability. What makes me sad is that we're brothers, we all belong to Eastern Europe. We've had a shared past, we were Communist companions for decades, our peoples rebelled against their dictators. The Romanians were more courageous than us: they killed Ceausescu and his wife in public, like wild dogs.

What can I say? This feud has been harmful to everyone. Think of our poor Italian clients—they're in a state of desperation. And what about our dear Italian junkie clients? They need cocaine to go to work and combat stress.

There are some who ask: why did the Romanians rebel against us? It's very simple. They became arrogant, even before Romania officially entered the European Union. They began to say: you Albanians are outside the E.U., you're not like us European citizens. They insulted us by saying that Albania isn't a European country. Albania *is* part of Europe! They decided to get rid of us so they could get their hands on everything. Drugs and prostitutes. Their numbers are greater than ours now: as we say in Albania, *Dy mace mundin nje ari*, two cats beat a bear!

There are also some who ask, justly, why the Romanians are so savage toward us. *Mir*, well, probably out of envy. They can't stand that the Albanians are real men, stallions. But it won't end here. The Albanians love vendettas. We in Albania have the Kanun, the law of revenge. It's no joke with us; a vendetta can last for centuries. Blood can be washed away only with blood. So the feud won't end soon.

I've never been arrested. The police don't have my fingerprints or my photo. I'm not an ex-con. I'm not so stupid as to turn to the forces of order. I don't want to have a record. I want to have a clean slate. I've applied for Italian citizenship and I'm waiting for a response. I'd also like to become a citizen of the E.U. I don't want to be outside it for my whole life.

Chapter 5
We're Not Provincial Anymore

I wake up reluctantly around seven. The phone won't stop ringing. As soon as I pick up the receiver I'm crushed by an avalanche of cries and words. I can barely grasp one phrase: "Patience, God give me patience."

"Enzu', what are you getting up to now?"

"Hi, Mamma."

"What's this business of the interview with Buscetta in today's paper?"

"Tommaso Buscetta died in 2000."

"That other one, the Albanian Buscetta."

"There's nothing to worry about, Mamma."

It's pointless to talk when your interlocutor doesn't listen. I decide to just take it, without responding. So then my mother becomes a verbal pugilist. She goes after me mercilessly. She pulls out her best arguments. For example, I'm thirty-seven years old and don't want to grow up. My contemporaries have wives and children and when am I going to have blessed child, eh? If I had one now there would always be an enormous age gap, almost forty years! If it were a girl it would be even worse, because I'd be leaning on a cane as I walked my future daughter to the altar. Whatever happens, I will always be an old father. Shit, now that I think about it, I guess I'll never be a grandfather. Then she talks about my cousin Pietro, who's only twenty-one. He's been married a year and he's already got twins. The kid, Pietro. A few years ago I could pick him up. What was the hurry to get married and have children? Instead of having fun like other guys his age. Ever since his goddam wedding my mother has been holding him up to me as an example. That bastard Pietro. In a few years he'll be able to go to a discotheque with his adolescent twins. Now he's enjoying being a dad, sooner or later he'll get tired of it and go back to being a kid. Another subject that never fails in my mother's rebukes: a home mortgage. She can't understand why I throw money away on rent when the majority of Italians own their own houses. The explanation is simple: I don't trust the banks and I don't like loans, alias debts.

"When a man has a wife and children he is more responsible."

"What am I doing wrong?"

"You're always out making trouble."

"I'm only doing my job."

"Now you've started writing about mafiosi! God give me patience!"

"You're getting upset about nothing, Mamma."

"I've given up, you're hopeless. But I was forgetting something important."

"What?"

"You've got to get a new bedspread."

"Why?"

"It should be thrown away, it's old."

"It doesn't seem that way to me."

"A woman sees things a man doesn't see. I already told Natalia to buy a new one."

"Yes, ma'am!"

I'm smart enough not to contradict her on the bedspread. My mother invents all sorts of things to remind me that I lack a permanent female presence, that is, a little wife. I decide not to go back to bed.

As I come out of my apartment I run into Aunt Quiz. She tells me that Joseph hasn't left the house for days. How can he live? It's a good question. But my aunt has an answer for everything, obviously. In her view, the African, as she calls him, has stockpiled food. So he can stay barricaded in his house for a long time. Aunt Quiz takes the occasion to dust off some memories. During the Second World War she suffered hunger; people ate everything, even cats. I decide to knock on Joseph's door. He opens it very cautiously. He lets me in quickly, and double-locks the door.

"What's all this mess, Joseph?"

"I don't know what to tell you, Enzo. They've accused me of taking Gino to the mosque. Can you understand it? Can you believe a thing like that?

"No."

"You've known me for years, I've never bothered anyone."

"That's true, but they say it was your pig."

"Where's the evidence?"

"It seems that it exists."

Joseph swears to me over and over that he and his Gino have nothing to do with it. Gino hasn't left his place on the balcony since he arrived, a month ago. Unfortunately now it's become dangerous to leave him out in the open. Joseph takes me to see Gino, whom, for the moment, he has settled in the bathroom. There's an intolerable stink. Yet the meeting with the piglet has its surprises. Gino is a Juventus fan: he wears a Juventus scarf around his neck.

To prove his innocence, Joseph plays all his cards. He has no reason to quarrel with the Muslims. In Nigeria, although he is a Catholic, he always had Muslim friends. He wouldn't dream of offending them. Apart from their different opinions on pork, Christians and Muslims in Nigeria share many things; for example polygamy—in fact Joseph's father has six wives. Finally, Joseph asks a favor.

"Enzo, help me talk to the guys at the mosque. I'd like to explain to them that Gino is innocent."

"I'll try, but it won't be easy. Do you intend to stay shut up in here?"

"I have no other choice. If I go out, they'll come and get Gino."

"And your job?"

He says he has completely changed his plans. He had been thinking of taking time off in December to go to Lagos and bring his wife and two children to Italy. After years he finally managed to get permission for his family to join him. Instead he has to take his vacation in advance to stay with his Gino. Joseph has lived in Turin since he came to Italy, in 1992. He's a couple of years younger than me, and he works in a hardware store near Piazza Statuto. He moved to San Salvario five years ago. We often watch the Juventus matches on Sky at my house.

"Enzo, please do something. Remember that Gino is a Juventus fan like us and we Juventus fans are all brothers, we have to help each other out."

"I'll do all I can for the Juventus piglet!"

We part with a warm embrace. I'm even more convinced of his innocence than before. Joseph is a little strange, but there are certain stupid things he wouldn't do. I'll go talk to the mosque guys. I hope I can settle this thing.

I pass by the newsstand and pick up the paper. My gaze falls immediately on my name, which is not alone; once again, Maritani joins me on the front page. The exposé continues. I go to Giacomo's café for breakfast. I read the headline and subhead: BEHIND THE SCENES OF THE FEUD. THE ALBANIAN BUSCETTA TELLS HIS STORY. Then the first lines:

> The secret source that shed light on the acts of violence of recent days comes out into the open and confesses to our paper. Continued on p. 2.

Next to it, on the left, I see Salvini's editorial. The headline is ambitious: WE'RE NOT PROVINCIAL ANYMORE. I skim through.

> Today this newspaper is publishing exclusive testimony. Our Deep Throat addresses the public directly. This is an absolute novelty in the history of journalism. In recent days some have compared our secret source to the Deep Throat of Watergate. This comparison fills us with pride and rewards our hard work. Nevertheless, in all fairness and intellectual honesty, we wish to point out that the American Deep Throat, Mark Felt, hid for more than thirty years, revealing his identity only last year, in 2005, while our source, the so-called Albanian Buscetta, has come forward after just three days. It's quite a difference. With respect and deep pride, we say: we are not provincial anymore.

I go to page two. In the middle there's a big photo of Tommaso Buscetta during his testimony at the maxi trial in Palermo in 1986. Naturally they couldn't publish a photo of the Albanian Buscetta. He's not available yet! I read the profile of Tommaso Buscetta.

> The boss of two worlds was born on July 13, 1928, in Palermo into a family of seventeen children. He hadn't even turned twenty when he joined the Mafia clan of Porta Nuova. In 1958 he was arrested for smuggling cigarettes. In the early sixties he left Italy for Mexico. Later he moved to the United States and then Brazil. In the seventies the Brazilian authorities agreed to the Italian request for extradition. After a few years of prison Buscetta was paroled and took advantage of that to flee. In the early eighties he returned to Sicily to fight the offensive against the Corleonesi, but without success. In this bloody feud he lost

many relatives, including two sons, whose bodies have never been found. He escaped to Brazil, where he was arrested in 1983 and again extradited to Italy. The next year he began to collaborate with Judge Giovanni Falcone. During the maxi trial against the Mafia in Palermo in 1986, he was heard as the principal witness. Making use of the laws favoring the *pentiti*, he spent his last years in the United States, with a new identity. He died in New York on April 2, 2000.

Afterward I read the testimony of the Albanian Buscetta. It's what I delivered to Maritani yesterday. He hasn't made any changes or additions.

At the café I order a cappuccino. I don't have time to enjoy my damn breakfast in peace when two men sit down without being invited. Apparently, rudeness is starting to spread even in San Salvario. I've known one of the men since I began reporting local news: Inspector Contini, of the homicide division of the Turin police. He's a real shit, he hates both journalists and southerners (and their descendants). He's also famous for being an incorrigible smoker, and in fact he doesn't give a damn about the ban on smoking in public places. For this he also deserves to be called the most arrogant man I've ever met. The second guy I've never seen before. He has a carefully groomed beard.

"What a coincidence, Laganà. I just happened to be passing by. I came with a colleague to do some shopping at the Madama Cristina market."

"You can save a lot there, inspector."

"The vegetables are very inexpensive. From now on, I'll always do my shopping here in San Salvario."

"Excellent decision."

"So we'll see each other often, Laganà. Who knows, maybe we'll finally even be friends."

"Friends? I'm afraid I'm not up to that, inspector."

Contini calls his informers "friends." He's tried it with me many times, and I've always told him to go to hell. After the preamble on shopping and vegetables, domestic nonsense, Contini moves on to more serious things. So I discover that the bearded man is a Romanian inspector who is collaborating with the Italian police under the auspices of a security agreement between Italy and Romania, which became operative at the beginning of the year. A Romanian cop in Turin! What's happening? Our police are importing a workforce from Romania?

"You want a cigarette, Laganà?"

"No, thanks. I don't smoke in bars."

"Good for you. I always try not to but I don't succeed."

"The important thing is not to give up, inspector."

The Romanian inspector intuits that we are circling around the question without getting to the point, so he intervenes to put an end to this game of cat and mouse.

"The situation is coming to a head, Mr. Laganà. Seven homicides in a few days. We don't know which fish to catch."

"That's not my business."

"We need a hand."

"I'm sorry, I can't. I have to protect my sources."

The words "protect my sources" enrage Contini. He can't contain his anger. He starts performing his favorite script, made up of shouts, provocations, and threats. I don't pay much attention; the dog that barks doesn't bite. What bothers me is this wretched scene taking place in public, in a bar frequented by people I know. That shit Contini is well aware of my weakness. I try, with great difficulty, not to fall into his trap.

"So you're comfortable among delinquents and criminals?"

"I'm a curious guy."

"Curiosity has nothing to do with it, Laganà. I think it's a family vice. By the way, how's your uncle?"

"He's fine and says hello."

Contini gets even angrier. The Romanian inspector tries to calm him down. A very difficult job. I decide to leave before the situation degenerates further. Uncle Carmine is my father's younger brother. He came to Turin as a very young man in the sixties. Instead of going to work at Fiat, like my father, he preferred organized crime, to the point where he became the boss of a clan of the 'ndrangheta. Now he's been a fugitive for ten years, after a conviction for association with the Mafia. I haven't seen him for seven years. There's an infinity of hypotheses on his hiding place: Germany, Spain, Scotland, Australia, Canada. And then some claim that he's never left Italy. The one thing for certain is that his "business" is booming, especially in money laundering. There's no shortage of front men among his fellow villagers—they exist in abundance.

I arrive at the newspaper at lunchtime. I get a warm welcome and lots of congratulations from my colleagues. For a local news reporter to make page one is a real achievement. Maritani looks for me; he wants to talk about something important. What else is he going to ask for? I go into his office. There's a poster for the film *All the President's Men*. It's right over his head. Next to it is the Padre Pio calendar and the poster of the 1989 Milan team.

"My dear Enzo, did you see the splash we made? We're in the national and international press reviews."

"Really?"

"Look here. You're quoted. You're becoming famous! Fantastic, don't you think?"

"You're right. It's really fantastic!"

Fantastic like hell. Shit, now I'm being exposed abroad, too! If I think about it, my Buscetta is yet another confirmation of the Thomas theorem: *If men define situations as real, they are real in their consequences*. In other words, it doesn't matter if a thing is true, people merely have to believe it's true for it to have real effects. The theorem was developed by the American sociologist William Thomas, an exponent of the Chicago School, in the late twenties. Thomas also wrote a very good book, about immigrants in America, *The Polish Peasant in Europe and America*. Working as a journalist, I've come to understand that the reality we confront has neither value nor weight. It's the imaginary that governs our actions or, rather, reactions. We are increasingly insecure, frightened, vulnerable, unreasonable. Someone should explain to me, for example, why the majority of Italians consider immigrants the primary cause of their lack of security when, at the same time, they entrust the persons dearest to them, children and old people, and the keys to their houses, to immigrant caretakers and housekeepers. What can be done? Must we be satisfied with a false, fleeting reality, devoid of concrete facts but loaded with fantasies and prejudices? Listen to me, with all these fine sociological observations, before long, I'll be giving Zygmunt Bauman a run for his money.

Maritani offers congratulations from the editor-in-chief, Salvini, who's going to be a guest tonight on *Rear Window*. Besides being the title of a famous Hitchcock film, it's also the name of the most popular talk show on Italian TV. The subject will be: immigration and public safety. In recent years our editor has worked hard to get back into the media limelight. And now he's succeeding in a big way. The years in the wilderness don't last forever. In the past he was very close to the socialists of Bettino Craxi and was considered one of the most powerful men in the media world. When he was at the RAI he acted like the owner, but following the Tangentopoli scandal he fell into disgrace.

"Enzo, a girl who works in films is coming in a little while. She wants to talk to you."

"What does she want from me?"

"I don't know, but try to make her happy."

"Why?"

Maritani gives me a few details. The girl's name is Sara Bertini, she's from a wealthy Turinese family. She was recommended by Salvini in person. Her father is the president of the Belpaese consortium, one of the biggest real-estate groups in northern Italy. Belpaese is also one of the most important advertisers in our paper. A few minutes later, as I'm surfing the Web, a really pretty girl stops in front of my desk. She has long hair, green eyes, and a voluptuous bosom. A real knockout. She's the girl Maritani told me about. So as not to be disturbed, I invite her to get a coffee at the bar downstairs from the office.

"You're doing a splendid job, Mr. Laganà. Congratulations!"

"Thank you."

"The story of the Albanian Buscetta is a real scoop."

"We do our best."

Sara tells me briefly what she does. She graduated in economics and has several master's degrees, collected in prestigious English and American universities. She specializes in television production but she also works in film. Three years ago she founded a production company, even though she's not even thirty. After the obligatory preliminaries she gets to the point.

"Mr. Laganà, I'd like to make you a job proposal, to work as a consultant for a TV miniseries."

"What's it about?"

The rich girl has definite ideas, she goes into the details with great flair. She explains that this story of the feud between Albanians and Romanians could be a good subject. She's thinking of a sort of *Octopus*—the great Mafia miniseries of the eighties. She has in mind the first series, the one directed by Damiano Damiani, with Michele Placido. "Ours" would be a non-European *Octopus*. And since, as a journalist, I know the world of foreign crime so well, she would like my help in writing the story and the screenplay. As for financing the project, there wouldn't be any problem. There's the family fortune, first and foremost.

"Thank you for the offer, but I'm really busy."

"It won't take much time, Mr. Laganà."

"I'm sorry."

"Could we meet again, to talk some more about it?"

"Of course. Maybe lunch?"

"Perfect, Mr. Laganà."

"Call me Enzo."

I agree to see her again not to impress Maritani but because I like her. And her job proposal? No, thanks. It doesn't interest me.

On the way home, I stop off at the mosque on Via Galliari. I know a lot of people who go there. Many of them have lived in San Salvario for years. I have a good relationship with Amin, one of the men in charge. He's a Tunisian political refugee, belonging to the Al Nahda party, which was declared illegal by the Ben Ali regime. He has a fruit-and-vegetable stall in the Madama Cristina market. I wait for Amin outside the mosque.

"What's all this with Joseph?"

"It's a nasty business, Enzo, he was disrespectful toward us."

"I talked to him this morning, he says he had nothing to do with it."

"He's a liar. The damn pig is his."

"Do you have evidence?"

Amin was expecting this question. He takes his laptop out of his backpack and shows me the video shot inside the mosque the night of the offense. A piglet with a scarf around its neck is clearly visible. The details don't escape me: it's a Juventus scarf. There's no doubt about it. It's Gino.

The video was sent to the e-mail address of the mosque the

next day. Amin tells me that the members of the mosque are extremely angry and want to teach Joseph a lesson. But he is doubtful about the use of violence. He's doing all he can to calm them down. To bring a pig into a mosque is a terrible desecration and creates a serious precedent. There has to be an energetic reaction, and without delay, to discourage possible imitators. Luckily, at the moment violence is only one of the options under consideration. They are sifting through other proposals, such as, for example, getting in touch with the satellite channel Al Jazeera and spreading the news on an international scale. There's the risk that Al Qaeda would get involved, and then, yes, that would be trouble. The consequences for San Salvario and Turin would be devastating. We all remember the Danish caricatures of the prophet Mohammed that showed a bomb in place of the turban, and the famous speech the Pope gave in that German university, when he claimed that Islam is synonymous with violence. The reactions were aggressive. In such matters Muslims don't play around. Churches were burned and the demonstrations lasted weeks. Another option would be to post Joseph's photograph and his address on the Internet. That would be more than enough to expose him in a big way and put his life in danger. There would be no need to offer a bounty, it would be sufficient to promise Paradise as the reward for whoever murders him. Joseph would be screwed, he'd have to live the rest of his life in hiding, and in constant fear of being murdered. He'd become a sort of Salman Rushdie. It would also endanger the lives of his relatives at home. Nigeria is a very complicated country, a real powder keg. It's not only the most corrupt country in the world; it's full of ethnic and religious conflicts. Violence between Christians and Muslims is always topical.

After the pig's "stroll" the mosque was unfit for use just for a morning, the time it took to clean it. Water was enough to purify everything. The damage to its image, however, is incalculable. Many of the faithful could pray in other mosques. But it's possible that the mosque of Via Galliari will be forever associated with the story of the piglet. Who knows, there might be people who, just to be offensive, will start calling it "the piglet mosque." This is unacceptable. If it came to that, it would be necessary to close the mosque and open a new one. But how and where? Today, especially after September 11, it's extremely hard to get the permits. Italians don't want a mosque next door, they think their property values will go down.

I didn't expect all these complications. It's a real minefield, it will be hard to get out of it undamaged. There is very little room to maneuver. But I can't leave Joseph alone, I promised to help him. I try to resolve the stalemate.

"Joseph wants to meet with you to explain his position," I say to Amin.

"There's nothing to explain."

"Let's try to find a solution," I persist.

"All right, then we have a proposal."

"Tell me."

"Joseph has to make a public apology."

"That's all?"

"No, it's not. He also has to give us the pig."

"I'll talk to Joseph and let you know."

Now I find myself right in the middle of a delicate negotiation. Why, I feel like nothing less than the secretary-general of the U.N.

After a dinner of steamed vegetables and lemon-roasted turkey, I sit down like a good housewife to watch TV. I've thought many times of getting rid of the television. But I always have second thoughts. I need it to watch films and old Juventus soccer matches on DVD.

Tonight there's a big event. The television audience will

finally behold the shitty face of Salvini, the editor-in-chief of our newspaper. Waiting for the start of *Rear Window*, I entertain myself by watching a special edition of *The Biscardi Trial.* A dozen guests, including journalists, actors, and politicians, comment on the weekend matches. Conducting the orchestra is Aldo Biscardi. This program has been on since the eighties. His *Don't all talk at once, at most two or three at a time!* makes me laugh. They're all shouting, trying to have the last word. They talk like fans and not like commentators. They're all super experts, in fact extreme experts. They know more than the coaches, the players, the referees, the managers. The trick is always the same: shout in order to keep your adversaries from talking. I think of the Milanese proverb that Maritani is always repeating, *Chi vusa püsè, la vaca l'é sua,* the one who shouts loudest gets the cow. I change the channel. The talk show is beginning. Here's the host, Severino Belli, alias Big Clown: "Tonight *Rear Window* is devoted to immigration and the security of our society, starting with the recent violence in Turin. A real feud between Albanian and Romanian criminals. Seven homicides in three days. The situation is dire."

The camera frames Salvini. A frightening closeup. Very elegant. Good presence. Arrogant face. Devilish smile. After the host's introductions, Salvini starts off with his long sermon. Romania will enter the E.U. at the start of next year. The stream of Romanians into Italy has increased out of all proportion. There are no precise statistics, but there are two very important facts: the first comes to us directly from the authorities in Bucharest, and that is that crime in Romania has gone down by fifty per cent. Second: the number of Romanian detainees in Italian prisons has risen precipitously in the past three months. The upshot? There's no doubt, there's been a flood of Romanian criminals into Italy. And if, before, the Romanians were outside the E.U., in three months they'll become citizens, and will be able to move easily. A bus ticket from Bucharest to Turin costs only sixty euros. Once they were affiliates of the Albanians, today they've gained strength numerically and financially. Therefore they want to work on their own. The stakes are the markets in drugs and prostitution.

Salvini defends the comparison with the First and Second Mafia Wars. There is a very clear criminal strategy. It's not a war between camorrists. The feud between the Lauro clan and the secessionists, for example, is a war of the desperate: the bosses are behind bars; there are no leaders, no well defined criminal strategy—there are only personal vendettas. Therefore, it's undeniable: the Romanians are the Corleonesi and the Albanians are the Palermo Mafia. And obviously he can't fail to mention the famous source.

"Dear Editor Salvini, there are some who have legitimate questions about your source. Does he really exist?"

"Of course he exists! In fact I've decided to make public a part of the recording of the interview."

"Mr. Salvini, thank you, and we're going to broadcast a preview. You'll hear for the first time the voice of the Albanian Buscetta. If we could have the recording, please."

The performance of Luciano alias the Albanian Buscetta deserves applause. He is terrific. After Salvini's speech the show loses its liveliness. The other guests, mostly politicians from different parties, are boring. The usual diatribe between majority and opposition. Here, too, it's just shouting and trying to keep the other guy from speaking, as on Biscardi's show. I think of that son of a bitch Salvini—he cleaned up. He has a natural presence, and he played his part brilliantly. A speech prepared down to the tiniest details. Simple words, clear concepts. Gray suit with blue tie. White shirt. Black designer shoes. Sitting with style. He looks like the Prince of Monaco!

At the end of the program they broadcast a clip from an old interview by the journalist Enzo Biagi with Tommaso Buscetta.

Then the whole debate centers on Buscetta's theory: Cosa Nostra is unique, it can't be compared to any criminal organization. Was the boss of two worlds right or wrong?

Chapter 6
Things Always Go That Way

I get up late. The alarm on my cell phone didn't go off. I forgot to charge it before going to sleep. I take care of that right away and while I'm still in bed I run through my pearls of wisdom. One cannot live today without the new technologies. We're constantly connected to the external world: too much, I would say. It's almost impossible to spend a moment of peace with oneself. We all have to be available, wherever we are; there's no way to detach ourselves from the collective torture. There are very few people who resist, who don't yet have a cell phone. They're considered maladjusted, lost sheep who will sooner or later return to the fold.

My reflections are abruptly interrupted by the arrival of an SMS: "Hello Laganà, you're on the wrong track. Follow Don Costantino Cassini. See you soon. Very Deep Throat." Is it a joke? The sender's number is strange. It was probably sent from some SMS site or from Skype. So it's impossible to trace the sender. I reread the message several times. The word "Follow," in English, is a reference to the Watergate Deep Throat when he puts the Washington *Post* journalist on the right track with the famous phrase "Follow the money." Why Don Costantino Cassini? He's a well-known figure in Turin, who's devoted his life to helping the needy, especially immigrants from Eastern Europe. I ought to have a chat with him—there would be nothing to lose. Maybe he can tell me something useful about the murders of the Albanians and Romanians. Priests are a real mine of information, which they intercept, exchange, and transmit constantly. An old Tunisian fisherman in Marseilles once said to me: "If you want to know a city quickly, go to the taxi drivers, the barbers, and the prostitutes." How could he have left out the priests?

I pay a visit to Joseph to try and persuade him to accept the proposal from Amin & brothers. A solution has to be found quickly. I find him tired and agitated. He hasn't been out of the house for days. He's like a prisoner. I tell him in minute detail about my meeting with Amin. He listens attentively, without interrupting. Finally I get to the point.

"To resolve the problem they ask for two simple things."

"What are they?"

"Apologize publicly and hand over the pig."

"I see that you don't believe in my innocence, Enzo."

"The problem is the others. It hardly counts if I believe you or not."

"I'll never hand over Gino."

"I don't see any other way out."

"It's not right. We're innocent."

Now Joseph is using a "we" that includes Gino and him.

"They have evidence that nails the pig," I insist.

"And what is this evidence?"

"They showed me a video of the pig in the mosque."

"It's false. Gino isn't the only pig on earth."

"There's no doubt, Joseph. The piglet in the video is yours."

Gradually Joseph begins to develop a conspiracy theory.

"Enzo, it's very clear. Someone wants to frame us, me and Gino."

"And who is that?"

"I don't know. But sooner or later I'll find out."

"Come on!"

Joseph won't even hear of handing over the piglet. An unacceptable proposal that stinks of betrayal. In these four weeks he has become very attached to Gino. They spend so much time together. Maybe they watch the Juventus matches together. My Nigerian friend divulges some facts that he has discovered during his cohabitation with the pig. For example, pigs are very intelligent, more than chimpanzees, dogs, or cats. They're sensitive, they can perceive joy and sadness in their masters. In other words, they seem like human beings. So he has decided not to eat pork anymore and not to use the word "pig" as an insult. As I listen to this stuff, I'm growing more and more convinced that poor Joseph is going out of his mind. I think this business had better end soon, in the interests of everyone. Otherwise, there will be trouble. Unfortunately my mediation isn't taking off, but I won't give up. I propose a meeting at my house with Amin & brothers as soon as possible. We have to confront the problem head on, face to face. He accepts, on condition that the meeting take place at his house. He doesn't want to leave Gino alone, he doesn't have confidence. He's afraid that someone will take advantage of his absence to kidnap Gino or, worse, kill him. I explain that that condition will be unacceptable: for the Muslims, the house is an impure place because of the piglet. So we're back where we started.

Irene Morbidi comes to see me at the paper. We've known each other since elementary school. She's always lived in San Salvario, not far from me, in Via Sant'Anselmo. To say that she adores animals is an understatement. They're her reason for living. Already in high school she and two friends formed an association to defend the rights of animals. From that moment on she has never stopped battling—the most recent fight was to close down a horse slaughterhouse. She is a fervent animal-rights activist.

"I heard that you're acting as a mediator between the

Nigerian and the people in the mosque about the piglet in Via Galliari. Is that true?

"Very true."

"We want to join the party."

"In what sense?"

"We want to adopt the pig."

"When it rains it pours."

All we needed was the animal-rights crowd! Irene tells me quite a few things. For example, the members of her group in Via Ormea, in San Salvario, have decided unanimously to adopt the piglet. Also, they've started an international campaign to save him. They've already got the first signatures; they expect that Brigitte Bardot will join, and likely be its godmother.

Irene rails against everyone, no one is spared. Joseph first of all, since he is keeping a poor little pig in horrible captivity. In other words, a pig in an apartment is unheard-of, a banal whim harmful to a defenseless animal can't be indulged. Then she moves on to the mosque. What more do they want? We've allowed them to open real laboratories of torture, called Islamic butchers. How many animals are cruelly slaughtered every day? Now they're angry with a pig? Hypocrites! Bunch of cowards. Then it's Mario Bellezza and his Masters in Our Own House committee. The fate of the pig doesn't interest them. What counts is feeding hatred toward immigrants. So a noble human and civic battle is in danger of being transformed into a spectacle of political propaganda. And what to say of the authorities, who don't lift a finger, in spite of the continual reports and protests? Irene warms up.

"We've had enough. We can't just look on. We have to do something."

"I'm doing all I can."

"Excuse me, Enzo, you don't understand that as a mediator you're becoming complicit?"

"Complicit in what?"

"If something happens to the pig, you'd be ethically responsible."

"And in your view what should I do?"

"Hand him over to us."

"That would complicate things even more, Irene."

"It's in the Nigerian's interest. Otherwise he risks prison or expulsion from Italy."

"Really!"

"Yes, we secretly made a long video of poor Gino when he was still on the balcony. We're sure that he's depressed because of his captivity. And you know what's the most serious thing?"

"What?"

"We saw that the Nigerian never gives him water. To deprive a living creature, man, animal, or plant, of water is the worst torture."

"But are you sure?"

Irene is absolutely sure. They've documented everything. I'll ask Joseph for an explanation next time I see him. At last, we arrive at blackmail, the famous either-or. Gino has to be handed over to the association Proud Animal Rights Activists, or the video of "torture by thirst" will end up on the desk of the relevant authorities. At that point, Joseph will be reported for mistreatment of an animal and will be in serious trouble. My negotiations have gotten even more complicated. Everyone wants Gino, but it's impossible to satisfy everyone.

Don Costantino is the priest of a small church in the Crocetta. I've known him for many years. He's about sixty, but he seems younger. He's always lively, with a pleasant smile stamped on his face. In addition to his regular duties, he manages an association that helps foreign detainees. Every week he goes to see them in jail and does all he can for them. To me he has always been cordial and accessible.

"Dear Enzo, this business of the murders is very ugly."
"It's a storm, Don Costantino."
"Storms leave ruin and destruction."
"Then we should try to limit the damage."
"By ourselves we'll never make it. We need the Lord."
"At least let's try, Don Costantino."

I make some coded remarks. Don Costantino is an intelligent person. I don't mention the SMS I got this morning; I let him talk about the general situation. The priest is really worried because of the murders, but more upsetting to him is the political and media campaign against the Romanians. There's a real danger of jeopardizing the imminent entry of Romania into the E.U. Voices have already been raised demanding that the great date be put off. Obviously it's a pretext for calling into question the whole process and nullifying the work that's been done so far.

Don Costantino tells me about the expectations of the Romanian immigrants who see their country's membership in the E.U. as a great opportunity. As European citizens they won't have to renew their residency permits. My reporter's instinct tells me that the priest has something important to reveal. In fact, after a little circling around, he comes out with it.

"Dear Enzo, we've known each other for a long time. In these years we've built a relationship of mutual trust and friendship, right?"

"Yes, absolutely, Don Costantino."

"Then I will take the liberty of telling you that what you've written about the Albanian-Romanian feud doesn't convince me at all."

"Why?"

"Can I trust you?"

"Of course."

Don Costantino talks to me about Florin Georgescu, one of the two Romanians killed last Sunday. He met him five years ago in jail and has kept track of him ever since. Anyway, he tried to help him, but unfortunately the Romanian was never able to get out of the circle of drugs and prostitution. He worked for a thug, a fellow Romanian. His task consisted of controlling and managing a group of prostitutes from the East.

Don Costantino gives me the background of his last meeting with Florin, the day before his tragic death. The Romanian was very agitated and feared for his life. He was afraid of being killed.

"By whom? The Albanians?"

"No, the Albanians have nothing to do with it. Enzo, the Albanian Buscetta has tricked you."

"And where is the truth?"

"Listen, Enzo, I can't reveal everything Florin told me during confession."

"I understand, but Florin is dead. Now the priority is to stop the terrible wave of killings."

"All right, let's make an agreement. I don't want to be quoted in any way. The Church has to remain outside of it."

"You have my word, Don Costantino."

Apparently, then, it was Italian criminals who killed Florin and his fellow-citizens. It was a punitive expedition. The Romanians didn't respect the agreement signed with the Italian criminal organization. They rebelled, thinking they were strong enough to impose new rules. Unfortunately, they made a big mistake. Probably the Albanians were killed for the same reasons.

"And what did Florin say about the Italians? Who are they?"

"He said only that they were from Calabria."

"Southerners, like me, but who are they?"

"A clan of the 'ndragheta."

"You can't be a little more specific, Don Costantino?"

"They belong to the Petri clan."

The Petri are not exactly complete newcomers. They're from Africo, in Calabria. In recent years they've grown more powerful, thanks to money laundering: liquidity is tempting to all entrepreneurs. It's also said that the Petri clan is the most formidable and well equipped on the military level. I thank Don Costantino for his time, and for the valuable information he's provided. As I head toward the car I see Contini. I hide so as not to run into him. After a few seconds I see him enter the same doorway I just came out of. He's here to talk to Don Costantino. Is he also on the right track?

I meet Sara Bertini in a restaurant near her office on Via Po. She looks great. She has a sensual smile that makes my head spin. We order a branzino with grilled vegetables for her and sea bream with salad for me. Sara takes a couple of DVDs out of her purse and offers them to me. I glance at the covers, which show Michele Placido with hair not yet white. But the writing is illegible.

"These are the versions of *The Octopus* in Russian and Japanese."

"I read somewhere that *The Octopus* is the most famous Italian TV series outside of Italy."

"Exactly. I have the complete collection in all languages."

"Really?"

Sara is an expert in the subject, a sort of *Octopus*-ologist. She explains that in Russia our Commissario Cattani, alias Placido, is a much loved star. In Japan he rivals Alain Delon. In Algeria, in the late eighties, the series was broadcast with the title *Mafia* during Ramadan. Millions of Algerians remained riveted to their TVs, deserting the mosques at evening prayers. Sara shows me some newspaper clippings. One in particular goes back a few years and discusses the responses provoked by former Prime Minister Silvio Berlusconi's statements during an official visit to Rome by Putin: "Before us, Italy was famous in the world for the series *Octopus*, but now it's a country to be reckoned with." Michele Placido responds: "I was sorry to hear the prime minister's words. It's true, I am the most popular Italian in Russia. Not me, but the character I played, Commissario Cattani, in whom the Russians have seen a clean and respectable Italian who fights the power of the Mafia. Could this be what annoys Prime Minister Berlusconi?"

"Enzo, our project can count on the international success of *The Octopus*. I'm sure I can find the necessary funding in Italy and abroad."

"Fantastic."

"We could aim at serial rights, make an Albanian, Romanian, Nigerian *Octopus* . . . What do you think?"

"Good project."

"When can we start the actual work?"

"Whenever you like. Let's meet for dinner in the next few days."

"O.K."

"People say I'm a good cook."

"Really?" I see that Sara is curious.

"Really. You want to come to my house for dinner?"

"O.K."

When I get to the office I find waiting for me the Romanian cop, the colleague of that son of a bitch Contini. I am struck this time, too, by the cut of his beard. An impeccable cut, I would say geometric. I invite him to take a seat in my office, a tiny room that I share with a colleague from the cultural page. The Romanian inspector is the opposite of Contini. He is cordial and very polite, a virtue that few cops possess.

"We didn't have a chance to introduce ourselves the other day."

"All the fault of your colleague."

"My name is Sandor Petriscu."

"Enzo Laganà, a pleasure."

"I don't want to waste your time. I came to ask you a favor."

"Please."

"Would you be so kind as to deliver a message to your source, the Albanian Buscetta?"

"What should I report?"

"He should turn himself in before it's too late. The circle is tightening. If he decided to collaborate it would be even better."

"He'll be in a protection program?"

"Yes, just like his predecessor, Tommaso Buscetta. Can I count on your mediation?"

"Of course."

We go on to talk about Romania and Romanian crime in Italy. Petriscu makes some sharp observations. For example, he explains that the Communist regime of Nicolae Ceausescu, like those in other countries of the East and the Third World, created immense open-air prisons. Distrust is the first rule of survival. It was said that half the society was spying on the other half. After the fall of Communism, people had only one desire: to get out! Young Romanians had inherited the "P syndrome": their *patria*, their native land, was a prison. No one wants to stay in Romania, everyone wants to get away, it doesn't matter where or how. The transition after Ceausescu wasn't successful. Once Communism fell, the new masters opened the gates to capitalism, and precisely to the negative aspects of the capitalist model, like consumerism. Fortunately, the goal of entering the E.U. generated a virtuous circle and a lot of enthusiasm. It forced the managing class to regulate itself, that is, to be at its best, by limiting its excesses.

The inspector explains why Romanians choose our country. For one thing, there exists a vast black market in labor, especially in construction and in elder care. For another, it's very easy to learn Italian. As for criminals, Italy is a much desired goal for them, too. They are very comfortable here, because the laws are permissive. Besides, it's not bad in Italian prisons the way it is in Romanian ones.

"What do you think the Italian government should do to rein in this crime?"

"I don't see any solution but expulsion. And that requires agreement with the Romanian authorities."

"So you're coöperating with the Italian police?"

"Yes, I arrived a month ago."

"You speak Italian perfectly. Where did you learn?"

"In Greci, a small village in the north of Romania."

"Italian is taught there?"

"Some descendants of Italian immigrants still live there."

"Really?"

Petriscu tells me a story that I've never heard or even read in history books, a story unknown to the overwhelming majority of Italians. At the end of the nineteenth century, thousands of Italians in the northwest emigrated to Romania to escape poverty, illness, hunger. Before the First World War, more than sixty thousand people from Friuli Venezia Giulia and the Veneto lived permanently in Romania. Italian laborers were very much in demand, above all in construction, as stonecutters, bricklayers, tile layers, carpenters, smiths . . . Petriscu's great-grandfather was originally from Treviso. During the Ceausescu regime it was forbidden to have Italian documents or to study Italian. Yet Petriscu's family was able to hand down the Italian language secretly from father to son, despite the risks.

"So do you have Italian citizenship?"

"Unfortunately no. All the documents that attest to our Italian origins both in Italy and in Romania have been lost. The only remaining proof is the language of Dante."

"That's too bad!"

Italian history is full of surprises. There are always new things to discover. I think that there does not exist a people stranger than ours. We Italians have not neglected any place in the world. We've gone everywhere, including to Romania to work as bricklayers. Today it's the Romanians who come to our country to do the same work. Irony of history.

In the evening Maritani calls to give me some important news. A young Romanian has been arrested. Apparently he is the serial killer of the feud. Can he really be guilty? Certainly this arrest will lessen the media and political pressure on the forces of order. Seven murders in a few days is a lot. That's why a culprit is needed, or at least a suspect, to feed to the public. Things are always like that.

Chapter 7
Prejudice Is an Incurable Disease

Today is the day for Natalia, alias spy No. 2. She comes once a week to clean, wash and iron the clothes, do the shopping, carry out tasks official and unofficial. She is a short, robust woman, around fifty, with a degree in chemistry. She has lived in Turin for eight years. She left two teen-age children and a husband in Kiev. Immigration from Ukraine is exclusively female, just as it is from the Philippines. Wives who emigrate leave the care of children to husbands and, above all, grandparents. A generation of orphans whose mothers are still alive. Natalia goes home only at Christmas. It was my mother who chose her, like all the housekeepers I've had. Obviously a perfect choice. There have been quite a few over the years. Later, Natalia will report everything in detail to her boss, as she does every week: how she found the house, a glance at the dirty clothes to get an idea of how I dressed during the past week, what's needed in the kitchen . . . My mother is very demanding, she wants answers full of particulars and opportunities for reflection.

Natalia likes to comment on the news, so she can't not talk about the feud between Romanians and Albanians. It's a subject that interests everyone, Italians and foreigners.

"Good Lord, these Romanians. What a terrible people."

"The Romanians are like everybody else, there are good ones and bad ones."

"The prisons are full of Romanians."

"The criminals are a minority."

"No. There are very many. Don't you watch TV?"

"You shouldn't trust TV."

"I don't trust Romanians."

"It's wrong to generalize, Natalia."

Try explaining to her, and, especially, persuading her, that the Romanians are Orthodox like her and that there are respectable Romanians with families to support and children to bring up. A life of sacrifices. I don't understand why there is no solidarity among colleagues, since the majority of Romanian women do domestic work. No way. Natalia can't stand the Romanians, it's impossible to make her change her ideas or at least sow some healthy doubts in her mind. The more I go on, the more convinced I am that prejudice is an incurable disease. There is no medicine or preventive measure that works. What can we do? Maybe we have to reluctantly accept living with prejudice. That likable genius Albert Einstein wasn't wrong: it's easier to split an atom than a prejudice.

I go to the café for breakfast. I take the opportunity for a quick glance at the various papers, put at the disposal of the customers. I should know what our competitors are saying. The headlines are all similar: ROMANIAN SERIAL KILLER ARRESTED. FEUD KILLER IN HANDCUFFS. A ROMANIAN CRIMINAL BEHIND BARS. ASSASSIN OF THE FEUD STOPPED. NON-EU KILLER STOPPED.

There's also a photograph. His name is Adrian Nicolescu, twenty-nine, he's been in Italy since 1999. I read here and there, in a disorderly way, searching for more details. But it's all in vain. I find the same nonsense, repeated, and simply reheated in various sauces. What bothers me most is the generalizing. The Romanian! The Romanians! The non-E.U. immigrant. Non-E.U. immigrants. The southerner! Southerners! What does it mean? Who are they? Why isn't an individual judged by what he does? Shouldn't the responsibility always be individual? After all, each of us goes to our grave individually, as a great North African saying puts it.

I take my newspaper and read Salvini's editorial. The title says it all: A CONTRIBUTION TO PUBLIC SAFETY. The beginning is enough.

> The forces of order have arrested a Romanian with a criminal record. He is accused of being the serial killer of the third Mafia war. We at our paper are happy to have contributed to this arrest, having been the first to reveal the criminal strategy in play. Our job, our primary duty, consists in informing the public.

Blah blah blah. An important detail is missing. All the papers say that the Romanian who was arrested has a criminal record, but they don't say any more, nothing specific, no explanation. What type of crime did he commit in the past? Robbery? Theft? Attempted murder? Extortion? Aggravated assault? International terrorism? Rape? Aiding and abetting prostitution? Drug dealing? These are crucial facts. My thoughts are suddenly interrupted by the arrival of the Romanian cop, Sandor Petriscu. He doesn't seem relaxed, as he was yesterday. He's not smiling anymore. What happened to him? Did his wife leave him? Was he denied a promotion? Did they steal his razor? Don't tell me he's already been infected by his fucking colleague Contini? Maybe he learned the Albanian Buscetta's response to the proposal of collaboration. Shit, he should give me the time necessary to carry out my mission as a mediator. Why is everyone in such a hurry?

"Do you have any idea who the Romanian they've arrested is?" he asks.

"Not yet, inspector."

"I, on the other hand, am sure that he has nothing to do with the events."

"What?"

"I saw him in jail yesterday evening during the interrogation. He has nothing to do with it."

"There seems to be evidence that pins it on him."

"No, only circumstantial. That's why they accused him only of the murder of the Albanians."

"And the other killings?"

"It will take time to find other perpetrators, I mean scapegoats."

"I read in the papers that he has a record."

"He was convicted a couple of years ago for assault. He punched his employer, who hadn't paid him for months."

"Now the picture is clearer."

Petriscu is angry with the journalists, a mass of unprofessional incompetents, who write a lot of bullshit without checking the facts. It's not right to throw a person onto the front pages, with photo, name, surname, country of origin. On this point it's difficult to defend my colleagues. Today, as everyone knows, sentences are handed down not in the courtroom but on newspaper pages and in television studios. And what is stamped in memory is the image of the arrest, not that of the release.

"Mr. Laganà, the boy is innocent and they want to frame him simply on the basis of your theory."

"What theory?"

"Your line of investigation into a feud between Albanians and Romanians."

"Come on, let's not exaggerate."

"It's the truth."

"Of course, now I'm the guilty one, dear inspector."

"Everyone must assume his own responsibilities."

"But what responsibilities?"

"There is an ethical code in all professions."

"I'm just doing my job as a journalist."

The Romanian cop goes away somewhat angrily. Never mind. How can you satisfy everyone? I don't understand his reasoning and I don't even want to know. What do I have to do with the arrest of the Romanian? If there is only circumstantial evidence, as he says, hence no proof or motives, the fault is the investigators', certainly not mine. Clear? Let him go somewhere else to give his little lesson on "assuming one's own responsibilities." Attempting to be totally honest with myself, though, I begin to have some doubts. A very small, goddam problem with my blessed conscience is emerging. What if the arrested Romanian is not the guilty one? And if my Albanian Buscetta was used to screw an innocent person? If that's the case, then it should be remedied right away, at the cost of inventing a "Thomas II theory." A really wild idea begins to buzz around somewhere else in my head. I immediately call Luciano Terni and we agree to meet at my house after dinner. If there's one thing that totally pisses me off it's a sense of guilt. I like to root it out at its origin.

As I get up to leave the café here's Mario Bellezza arriving. He's out of breath. Why all this hurry?

"Enzo, is it true that Gino will be handed over to the shits at the mosque?"

"There's no agreement yet."

"Then you confirm that negotiations are under way?"

"Yes, we're looking for a solution."

"And us? Don't we count for a goddam thing?"

"Who said that?"

"Why were we excluded?"

"Nobody's been excluded."

It takes some time to calm him down. A nice cold beer might put him at his ease. Too bad he doesn't like to drink in the morning. Damn, what I have to do! If it keeps going like this I'm changing careers. Maybe I should be the neighborhood psychologist.

Bellezza shows me a series of flyers. Right in the middle of each one is the image of a piglet wearing a green scarf. The captions, however, vary: Don't touch Gino! Gino is one of us! All for Gino! Hands off Gino! Gino the Italian piglet! Gino the very Italian piglet! Gino a piglet of the Po!

Bellezza takes the opportunity to update me on some things. For example, the local committee, the famous Masters in Our Own House, of which he is the president, has decided unanimously to guarantee protection to Gino, in other words to give him a sort of political asylum. Gino the pig, the first animal political refugee in history. Over the next days a great mobilization will begin on his behalf, not only in San Salvario but in all Turin. The voice of the natives must be heard. Mario Bellezza uses the very word "natives." I have to admit that it has a strange effect to hear it from the mouth of a person like him, a *terrone*, a southerner. And by the way, what happened to the word *terrone*, meaning, literally, covered with dirt? How did it disappear from daily language? Maybe it's been replaced by "non-E.U."? Bellezza keeps harping on the same thing: the immigrants have to understand, once and for all, that here in our house they cannot command. Then he ups the ante a bit, warning me against handing Gino over to the Muslims. If he is killed according to Islamic ritual, as they have announced, there will be hell to pay. I try to slow down this raving.

"Who said the pig will be killed according to Islamic ritual?" I ask.

"The people from the mosque."

"I don't think I heard that."

"They'll certainly kill him."

"Slaughtering according to Islamic ritual is a whole other thing," I explain patiently.

"Enzo, we've decided to seize Gino by any possible means."

"The priority is to get Joseph out of trouble—he's in danger."

"We don't give a damn about the African."

"I knew that from the start."

Poor Joseph is worth less than a piglet. For Bellezza and his damn committee, the important thing is not to lose face. Now they've stuck out their necks on behalf of the pig and against the Muslims. Here I am, then, facing another ultimatum. Maybe the solution is to clone Gino. That's the only way I can satisfy all the contenders.

"Gino is now under our protection. Anyone who touches him is in trouble," Bellezza resumes.

"Threats are useless."

"We're exasperated, Enzo."

"You need more common sense."

"We're willing to ransom him. How much does the African want?"

"Joseph doesn't want to sell him."

"The Nigerian has already been enough of a pain in the ass. He can't always do what he wants. Make him see reason, Enzo."

"I'll try."

The negotiations are at a dead end. I don't see a solution, at least for the moment. Maybe we should give up? I'm sorry for Joseph. I don't know how he'll get out of this unharmed. I get an SMS: "Dear Laganà, Follow Professor Alberto Lanzino. You'll find him every afternoon at the central city library. See you soon. Very Deep Throat." An SMS identical to the other one. Sender unknown. Why Lanzino? As far as I know, he's an urban sociologist who taught at the University of Turin before being expelled in a nasty harassment scandal. He was accused by a couple of students a year ago. But what does this professor have to do with the murder of Albanians and Romanians? Anyway, it could be useful to have a few words with him. The previous SMS had results. Very Deep Throat didn't mislead me or waste my time. The trail of the priest was good. Let's see where the trail of the professor leads.

*

Luciano arrives a little before midnight. He's a very smart guy, even if he's always looking for confirmation of his gifts. I don't know exactly why. Maybe he's a little insecure and wants to be reassured. Or he's simply an artist and, like all artists, needs to satisfy his own narcissism. Anyway, I'm very generous with compliments on his terrific performances.

"I'm glad you liked the Albanian Buscetta."

"Luciano, you were fantastic."

"One always has to aim high, Enzo."

"Never be satisfied."

"Exactly."

"You're a brilliant artist."

Luciano explains some details. To prepare for the part, he worked like a real professional. His artistic method is based on the following principle: a lot of study, a little improvisation. He consulted with Albanian friends of his from Durrës, obviously without revealing our secret: he explained his interest by saying that he was getting ready for a show about immigrants. He collected proverbs, swear words, and other phrases in the original language. Then he recorded their voices, and worked till dawn to perfect his pronunciation.

"You know, Enzo, I found it hilarious when *Rear Window* broadcast the voice of the Albanian Buscetta."

"I really had a good laugh. You sounded just like an Albanian."

"Right now I'm imagining you sitting in that shitty television studio. You want a taste?" Luciano says excitedly.

"Sure."

"Good evening, ladies and gentlemen. I am your beloved host Severino Belli. And, as I've done almost every night for many years, I come into your houses without permission, in fact into your bedrooms and under your covers, not to inform you but to stick it up your ass. Tonight we have invited the greatest crime reporter in Italy. Please, Mr. Laganà, have a seat. Would you like a blow job right now or after the show?"

"Fantastic imitation! Bravo Luciano. Now we have to enrich the repertory."

"Another performance with the Albanian Buscetta?"

"No, a new role."

I explain to Luciano my idea about the new character. He should be a cross between a Romanian criminal and Totò Riina or Leoluca Bagarella. For artistic inspiration there is an embarrassment of choices in the many films on the rise and fall of the mafiosi. Our character is a ruthless assassin who admits that he is the killer of the Albanians.

"It will be like the other time, I'll be there with Maritani. We'll ask you some questions about your criminal career. You should be very insistent about the code of honor."

"In the sense that I'm not an ordinary criminal but a boss?"

"Exactly! Try to explain that the killing of the Albanians is a vendetta."

"Something like: for years they've fucked our girls?"

"It's not enough as a motive. You could add that they've have been acting like bosses, treating the Romanians like servants."

"OK. I can also say I hate the Albanians because they're Muslims."

"Excellent idea."

Before he goes we agree on other details: this time, too, the compensation will be given to charity and Luciano will follow the same method of preparation he used for the Albanian Buscetta. So he'll go have a chat with some Romanian immigrants, looking for idioms, phrases in the language, and general information about Romania. Tomorrow afternoon he'll make his official début in another show. Will he succeed as well as he did the first time?

Chapter 8
The Hand That Infests Is the Same That Decontaminates

Wives who are a pain in the neck always live longer. It's not a male-chauvinist saying: a serious scientific study published by a famous American university says so. The explanation is simple. The heart is a very delicate organ, it needs an outlet. The danger is holding everything inside. Sooner or later the poor heart can't take it, and then what happens? It stops functioning and the whole body breaks down. Women are very good at getting rid of evil thoughts and ugly feelings. Never mind if it's the poor men—husbands, companions, and boyfriends—who pay the bill.

Giacomo the barman is perfectly in agreement, and to confirm the reliability of the research he draws up a list of the oldest widows in San Salvario, who live in happiness and tranquility thanks to the pensions of their deceased husbands. Aunt Quiz doesn't agree, she feels impugned. She doesn't accept the insinuation. In other words, it's like claiming that her longevity is the result of the complaints she inflicted on her dead husband. A small malicious murderer. That is really unacceptable. She launches into a series of observations that go from traditional to modern medicine. She demonstrates her knowledge of the subject, picked up in many years of quiz shows and television programs. Giacomo retreats, not having the same scientific or, especially, television expertise. I don't want to take a position and, as a result, annoy one of them. It's better to be a spectator.

While I'm enjoying the show Amin arrives. I buy him a coffee. We start talking about politics and soccer. Luckily we move on to more serious things right away.

"Has the Nigerian accepted our offer?" he asks.

"No, unfortunately."

"Then I'm truly sorry. We've done our part. Now I can't guarantee anything."

"What's going to happen?"

"*Allah alam*, only God knows."

"But he wants to meet with you to explain things."

"What's the use of talking?"

"To find a solution," I insist.

"First he has to apologize."

"Joseph continues to repeat that he is innocent."

"He's a coward, not an innocent."

"He's a good person, we've known him for years," I remind him.

"Maybe he was paid or manipulated by someone."

"Who would that be?"

"I don't know, it's only a hypothesis. Anyway there's no lack of enemies in San Salvario."

Amin's allusion leads directly to Mario Bellezza and his committee. The deadlock has not been broken. It's hard to make each side reconsider its position. At a certain point Amin discloses some confidential information. For instance, heated arguments are going on among the brothers of the mosque, on various subjects. What is the best way to intervene and resolve the problem of the piglet? Should the solution be peaceful or violent? There are some who have faith in my mediation, but there are others, real hotheads, who are calling for the use of force. They say they should seize the piglet and teach the Nigerian a good lesson. A punitive expedition. The second argument is strictly religious. The pig, of course, is impure for Muslims, who are forbidden even to touch it. The question is this: how to kill the pig without touching it? So maybe it has to be shot at close range, but using a firearm in an apartment would be extremely dangerous. Another argument has to do with the advisability of resorting to the law. There are some who say they should turn to the courts. Italy, after all, is a civilized country. Many of them, however, don't believe in Italian justice. Since the attacks of September 11th, it hasn't been easy for a Muslim to win a legal case. Others push in the direction of the media. They should take their case to the media and gain people's sympathy. It's a way of putting pressure on the local authorities so that they will allow the Muslims of San Salvario in particular and of Turin in general to have decent mosques and not makeshift places to pray. But the result could be counterproductive. In a battle against a pig, the Muslims run the risk of losing the support of public opinion. Italians love animals, including pigs, more than Muslims. In other words, there are people like Mario Bellezza who consider the pig a true cultural symbol, like the cross in schools. So a match against the piglet will be lost before it begins.

Amin, unburdening himself, tells me a big secret: during the last meeting in the mosque they decided to ask the Egyptian and Saudi religious authorities to impose a fatwa, a religious sentence. How should the matter of the piglet be resolved? They have to wait for a response. So it will take time. I myself certainly won't complain about possible delays. The greatest jurists of Islam surely have more urgent questions to discuss. Gino is creating controversies on top of controversies, disputes on top of disputes. Before we part, Amin offers another proposal to get the negotiations off the ground.

"Enzo, we're willing to give up the handing over of the piglet."

"And what do you want in exchange?"

"We want it out of San Salvario as soon as possible."

"That seems like a good step forward."

"That will be the last concession."

"Thanks for your willingness, Amin. I'll let you know."

Finally a glimmer of light in this tunnel—I see a small way out. We need some common sense. No mediation can be successful without concessions from the contending parties. On my side, I've done everything possible, I'm doing the impossible, and as for miracles others will have to take care of those.

In the late morning I drop in at the main city library, just around the corner from the paper. I find Professor Alberto Lanzino on the ground floor, in the reading room with the Italian and foreign newspapers and magazines. He's a man in his sixties, thin, with grizzled hair, well dressed, in a gray suit and red tie. I go over and introduce myself. I have the impression that my name isn't completely unknown to him. Maybe he's read the bullshit that's been published about the feud. It's not easy to explain the reason for my visit, so I try to invent one on the spot. I play it safe, to avoid a gaffe.

"Professor Lanzino, I'm doing a small report on how criminal elements from abroad are transforming our city."

"And how can I be of use to you?"

"I'm interested in your point of view as an urban sociologist."

"Lately it's journalists doing stories on gossip, on harassment, who've been bothering me."

"I followed that business you were involved in, and I have to say that the students' story wasn't completely convincing."

"They did all they could to discredit me, but I'm a hard nut."

"Sooner or later the truth will come out."

"The girls were simply used as pawns. The real problem is those who were behind it, just like in that business of the third Mafia war that you're following."

"Could you be clearer, professor?"

"Would you mind if we go outside?"

"Of course, it will be quieter."

Professor Lanzino doesn't waste time asking for a guarantee of anonymity, like Don Costantino. He begins his speech with a question, as he might do with his students at the university.

"You know what gentrification is?"

"Yes."

"It's the key to understanding everything that's happening."

"In what sense, professor?"

Lanzino is really good at explaining theories and concepts. He's had many years of teaching. So this damn gentrification is a concept that was used for the first time by the English sociologist Ruth Glass to study certain poor neighborhoods of London. It indicates the transformation of a run-down neighborhood into a residential area, following a process of improvement and renovation. The first consequence is an immediate rise in property values as the poor are moved out into deteriorating neighborhoods. Besides the economic benefit, there exists a political benefit in terms of image for the local authorities. In other words, it's always a good card to play during election campaigns. Obviously, there is no shortage of catchy slogans: "Urban renewal," "Safer neighborhoods," "Livability and development," and blah blah blah.

Postindustrial cities offer great opportunities for this process of gentrification. There's been a lot of talk lately about the city of Detroit, following the crisis of the automobile industry. Turin isn't very different from Detroit, because of Fiat's troubles. According to Professor Lanzino, if gentrification is a normal and spontaneous phenomenon in cities like London and post-unification Berlin, for others, like Turin, the situation is complex and full of unknowns.

"You mean you can recognize the hand of organized crime?"

"I have no doubt. Gentrification is encouraged here."

"In what sense, professor?"

"The gentrification process I've studied in Turin has led me to examine more closely a new phenomenon: the 'rats' nest.'"

"What do rats have to do with it?"

"They represent a first-rate model of reference."

"I don't understand."

"The rats' nest neighborhoods are first infested by various forms of crime and then are decontaminated. The hand that infests them is the same that decontaminates."

"I'm beginning to understand."

Professor Lanzino gets into details. In recent years, the 'ndrangheta, the most dangerous criminal organization in the world, has intensified its money-laundering activities in the north of Italy, by investing in real estate. Since the criminal mind is fertile and creative, the criminals have put into practice a plan that consists of "infesting" certain neighborhoods in Milan and Turin, by bringing in prostitutes and drug dealers. That's when the 'ndrangheta buy up all the property they can. In the second phase they proceed to the cleanup, moving the "rats" elsewhere and creating trendy places for all tastes: students, singles, young people, professionals, gays . . . The prices of the houses increase. The 'ndrangheta understands perfectly that Italians don't trust banks, they have faith only in brick. And there you have it! For the clan it's extremely important to find new pathways for money laundering. In this criminal picture, murder is an important option for imposing its dominance.

"I hope my analysis is clearer now."

"On the theoretical plane it's very clear, professor."

"The practical plane fits perfectly with the theoretical."

"But is there any hard proof?"

The word "proof" enrages the professor. According to him, transforming "possible evidence" into "proof" depends only on the seriousness of the institutions and the maturity of civic society. The real challenge isn't a lack of evidence, partly because there is tons of evidence, but fighting the collusion with organized crime. A few years ago, a minister of our Republic let slip an incredible statement: it would be useful to find a basis for living together with organized crime! The rats' nest phenomenon is not an invention but a reality, in Turin and other Italian cities. The professor has developed a map of neighborhoods that have been infested and then decontaminated. The four Albanians and three Romanians killed were used as "rats," it's no coincidence that their bodies were found precisely in neighborhoods that were recently infested and are now being decontaminated.

"Who's behind those murders, professor?"

"Identifying the principals is always complicated, but not impossible."

"You can't be more explicit?"

"They've already ruined my reputation. Next time they'll kill me."

"Who?"

"I've already said enough."

"I understand perfectly, professor, but I need to have confirmation for information that I get from a single source."

"I want to stay out of this business."

"I'll guarantee you anonymity. Let's proceed like this: I'll ask you a question, if you don't answer I'll take it as a confirmation. OK?"

"Fine."

"Is the hand of the Petri clan behind it?"

". . ."

Fantastic! The trick used by Woodward and Bernstein to get confirmation from a Watergate witness has worked perfectly. I thank Professor Lanzino for his invaluable help. Now I have to organize the various pieces of information I've got. It seems to me that the rats' nest plan is the motive. The murdered Albanians and Romanians were the infesting rats. This time, too, the mysterious Very Deep Throat has not disappointed me.

Before going to see Maritani, I relieve the tension a little by smoking a cigarette. I put my ideas in order, a bunch of crap about Deep Throat II.

"Angelo, we have another source."

"Another Deep Throat?"

"Yes, Deep Throat II."

"So let's get an update: Washington *Post* 1–our newspaper 2! I'm listening, Enzo."

"The Romanian who was arrested the other day is innocent."

"How do you know?"

"I'm in contact with the real killer."

"And who is he?"

"A Romanian boss."

Maritani is very happy. It's yet another confirmation of his brilliant theory, according to which the Albanians are like the Palermo Mob, the losers, while the Romanians are like the Corleonesi, that is, the winners. The 'ndrangheta, too, had its feuds and internal wars. Between 1985 and 1991 more than seven hundred people were killed. My editor has a weakness for the Sicilian Mafia: he's very inspired, and in fact he develops his theory further: the Romanian boss is a sort of Totò Riina. So he wants to call Deep Throat II the Romanian Riina. I have no comment, so as not to raise doubts about the famous third Mafia war. If there is one thing that pisses me off it's to see my colleagues make banal and stupid comparisons, equating facts, places, and persons that have nothing to do with one another. Every situation is unique, even if analogies exist. Arranging the practical details of the interview is child's play. We simply follow literally the script of the Albanian Buscetta: same time, same location, and same compensation. The birth of the Romanian Riina is simple, there are no complications, but I have to concentrate in order not to make a mistake. The game is getting rough. It takes great mental power to manage not one but two deep throats at the same time.

If you saw us, Maritani and me, sitting at the old kitchen table in an uninhabited apartment, we'd look like two idiots at a séance. Luckily, Maritani has brought a thermos of coffee and some cookies. At a certain point the table begins to tremble. With the vibration the cell phone makes a little pirouette. Finally we are in contact with the mysterious voice, thanks to speaker phone.

"Hello, it's Laganà."

"Dear sir, it's me. How is everything?"

"All fine. I'm with the editor, Maritani."

"Dear Mr. Maritani, what a pleasure to meet you telephonically."

"The pleasure is mine. I would like to thank you warmly in the name of my newspaper for your availability. Tell us, what shall we call you?"

"Call me Tigru, in Romanian it means Tiger."

"Fine, Mr. Tigru. How shall we introduce you to our readers?"

"I'm an entrepreneur, a businessman living in Italy."

"What type of business do you do?"

"Import-export."

"In what sector? Can you be more precise, Mr. Tigru?"

"Well, I import into Italy the most valuable commodity in the world."

"Which is?"

"*Pizdă.*"

"Excuse my ignorance, what product is that?"

"Pussy, dear sir! Italian males can have it for the price of a pizza. They even rhyme, *pizdă* and pizza."

"A low-cost product."

"Bravo, Mr. Maritani. I like 'low-cost pussy' a lot. You know what my advertising slogan is?"

"Tell us."

"*Pizdă* for all!"

I leave to Maritani the job of asking the questions while I enjoy the answers of Luciano, alias Tigru, in silence. Every so often I feel like laughing, but I resist the temptation. There's no doubt about it, the performance is magnificent.

After the interview, Maritani gives me two jobs. First: transcribe the story of Tigru, or the Romanian Riina, as he calls him, in the form of a first-person narrative, taking out all the swear words. Second: prepare a biographical profile of Totò Riina. It won't be hard to get the relevant information on the Internet.

I spend the evening at Biberon. By now the club has become Sam's headquarters. We sit down with a couple of beers.

"How's your mediation about the pig going?"

"Improving."

I summarize for Sam. It's also a chance for me to assess the situation. There are too many players in this game and they all want to be in charge. Poor Gino's going to end up as the ball.

"You know what I think about this business, Enzo? There's only one way out."

"Go ahead."

"Joseph should convert to Islam. That way no one can touch him."

"Don't be ridiculous."

"To save his ass. Isn't it better to be converted than to be killed?"

"And what about Gino, can he convert?"

"Unfortunately Gino is screwed."

"Can you explain it? Why do you Muslims have such a thing about pigs?"

"They're *haram*, strictly forbidden in Islam."

"I know that. Jews don't eat pork, either. But let's talk about you."

"What do you want from me?"

"You don't eat pork, but at the same time you drink all kinds of alcohol and you fuck right and left. That's also *haram*."

"The pig is disgusting because it eats everything, including shit."

"So do chickens."

"I don't know what to tell you."

"Can't you be more convincing," I press him.

"Are you now the spokesman for Mario Bellezza and his lousy committee?"

"Try to be more consistent with your religion and don't be a pain in the ass."

We discuss pigs for a long time but without solving the real problem. Sam tells me an anecdote: an Egyptian took over a bread bakery in San Salvario. To get his business going and attract customers he began to spread the idea that Italian bakers use pig fat in their dough. The ruse worked in a big way. Can one say there exists such a thing as pig-phobia? I think so. I remember a short film from the postwar period by Michelangelo Antonioni on the street cleaners of Rome. There's a scene in which the garbage that's been collected and ground up is given as food to pigs. Those images are stamped in my memory.

Chapter 9
Low-Cost Sex or *Pizdă* for All

My name is Tigru, I'm forty-six years old. I was born in Bucharest, the capital of Romania, so I'm not a wretched peasant like the people who come from the countryside. I have a middle-school diploma. I committed my first murder at sixteen, but luckily no one found out. I've been in jail many times, but for short periods. *Inchisoarea este o scoala importanta,* prison is an important school. It's indispensable for our profession. In other words, you have to learn from people with more experience. I have to say that I'm very grateful to my teachers. In prison there's a lot of theory and not much practice. Each time I got out, I put into practice everything I'd learned. Luck counts, but opportunity counts more. I always tried to take advantage of every one.

I began working for a boss in Bucharest, right after the fall of the Communist regime. Little by little I became a trusted lieutenant, then, after I married his daughter, his right-hand man. We made a lot of money. Ours is a difficult profession. *Banii*, money, never walks together with the law. Money has absolute power. Money is a magic key that opens all doors. It was extremely easy to corrupt everyone in Romania, from politicians to bureaucrats, from journalists to cops, from public officials to judges. At a certain point, Romania became too small for us, we had grand ambitions. We carried out great plans to expand our activities. So we came to Italy.

De ce Italy? Why Italy? I don't understand why I'm always asked that question. The answer is obvious. Italy is a very beautiful country, there are very beautiful women, and above all there's a lot of money. We're in your country for business, import-export. Our Italian colleagues, like the Mafia, the Casalesi, and other clans, come to invest in Romania and all over the world, the Romanians come to invest in Italy. *Care este problema*? What's the problem? This is called capitalism, or am I wrong? Money is free to go where it wants. I'm sure things will be even better for everyone after Romania enters the E.U.

I often hear it said that Italian businessmen go to Romania to start up businesses, to give work to my fellow-citizens. In other words, they bring well-being to my country. We, too, import well-being to Italy. We import the most precious commodity in the world: sex! Italian men can have sex at a low price, only ten euros. The price of a pizza! Not only the rich can have a fresh, pretty girl available to them. Also the less rich can enjoy when they want and where they want. Our motto is: Sex for all! This is real communism, equality among all the males in the world.

There are some who claim that we don't respect your laws. *Este adevarat*, it's true. I don't like to deny the evidence. The first lesson I learned at the start of my career is: doing business means fuck the laws. As for Romania, by this point it's a small Italian colony. In many areas the language of business is the Veneto dialect. Many Italian businessmen do as they like: they don't pay taxes, they don't give a fuck about the unions, and they dump the waste from their factories wherever. They make a lot of money, and there's nothing left for the Romanians.

I, as a foreign businessman in the sex industry, reject the label of criminal. Let's be serious, others are criminals, not people like me. To me it's racism, discrimination, envy. Allow me to get something off my chest. I often hear immigrants complaining about the lack of integration in Italy. I don't agree. My industry is perfectly integrated into Italian society, just like the Mafia, the Camorra, the 'ndrangheta. It's not right to say that immigrants can't be integrated in Italy. I have to admit that I worked hard. You have to sweat for integration. For example, I watch *The Godfather* once a year to get inspiration and to learn. I really identify with the character of Don Vito Corleone. My great dream is to go and live for a while in Corleone. It will be more complicated now; I have to be careful not to attract attention.

Let's get to this feud between us and the Albanians. The Albanian Buscetta told your newspaper that we Romanians were ungrateful. It's not absolutely true. We were clever. Those are two different things. As we say among ourselves: *sa te faci frate cu dracul pana treci puntea,* be a brother to the devil to get across the bridge. The Albanians are Muslims; we Romanians are Christians. By definition we can't get along. There's a clash of civilizations, a religious war. We're very different. They're like the Turks, they don't belong to Europe. We are about to become citizens of the E.U. and they will be outside it forever.

Finally, I would like to be clear on an important point: I killed only the Albanians, so I confess to four murders. It wasn't me who killed the others. I swear on the head of my mamma. As for the future? The feud will continue. We are the stronger. This is our chance to become the bosses. We will be ready. What do we want? It's simple: we want the world and everything in it, as Tony Montana said in *Scarface. Multi multumiri*, many thanks.

CHAPTER 10
A SECOND-GENERATION SOUTHERNER

I get out of bed as if I were blind drunk. I have just one desire: silence the continuous ringing of that damn telephone. I pick up the receiver and a storm of words rushes at me.

"Enzu', now what are you doing to me?"

"Hello, Mamma."

"God give me patience."

"Mamma, what's the matter?"

"What's this interview with the Mafia boss Riina?"

"What are you talking about? Riina is in prison under Article 41 bis, he can't give interviews or see journalists."

"I meant the other one, the Romanian Riina."

"It's a newspaper story. You know how the papers always exaggerate. Calm down, Mamma."

"I can't calm down as long as you insist on associating with gangsters and pirates. You're ruining my health."

"Come on, Mamma!"

"Listen, I was forgetting. There's a lot of salad in the fridge—did you eat it?"

"Yes, but not all."

"Look, the expiration date is the day after tomorrow. Then there's a problem with the vase outside."

"What vase?"

"The one on the balcony. Someone moved it."

"So?"

"Put it back where it was before, on the left. Where it is it could fall on the head of some poor unfortunate."

"It will be done, yes, ma'am."

I wish someone would explain something to me: where does my mother find the time to worry about the refrigerator in my kitchen, not to mention the vase on my balcony? I've never come up with a convincing answer. How does she do it? Hell, she doesn't live around the corner from San Salvario, she lives in Cosenza. But you have to admit that she's a genius of household management. She hates waste, especially when it comes to food. For her, food is sacred. Before she buys anything, she thinks at least a hundred times. She could become an anti-waste, pro-sustainable-growth guru.

I take a shower and shave and decide to go up to Joseph's. Yesterday evening he called, wanting to see me urgently. I hope he's had second thoughts and will agree to hand over Gino.

"I've discovered who wants to frame us, me and Gino."

"Who?"

"The Toro Ultras. I'm sure."

"Soccer fans? Come on!"

"Ever since Juventus ended up in Series B we've become easy targets for everyone. No one respects us anymore."

"But what does soccer have to do with this?"

Joseph tries to convince me that maybe it's a joke, a nasty joke on two Juventus fans, that is, him and his Gino. Why was only Juventus punished? Why did Milan, Inter, Lazio, and the other teams come out of it unscathed? I have to admit that this conversation gets to my black-and-white Juventus pride.

"Enzo, I'd like to ask a big favor."

"What?"

"Get in touch right away with the Juventus Ultras."

"Why?"

"To ask for help. Gino and I can't make it on our own."

"It's not a good idea, Joseph."

I try to convince him that we need a peaceful solution. Among the fans are a lot of hotheads, ready for violence.

Especially this year, with Juve in Series B. They'll seize on any pretext for an outburst, to avenge the great injustice that was done. In the end it will be poor Gino who pays. The situation is already tense. A match is all that's needed to start an uncontainable fire.

Joseph has become paranoid, and so the worst is yet to come. I also have to reckon with lunacy.

"By the way, Joseph, is it true that you don't give the pig water?"

"Yes."

"Why?"

"The animal doesn't need water."

"You're sure?"

"Very sure. The grass quenches his thirst directly, he retains the liquids. So I always have a lot of fresh fodder for Gino."

"Who told you that?"

"That's how we do it in Africa."

"Then you really are nuts."

In Los Angeles there are no pedestrian crossings. And so how do the poor pedestrians manage, especially the old ones? Aunt Quiz is very worried, she's afraid of getting hit by a car. Giacomo the barman, as usual, can't mind his own business: "What do you care about Los Angeles, whether they have crossings or not?" My aunt's response is always ready: "I have every reason for knowing this important information in advance. I have to be careful to avoid being swindled in the future." Giacomo won't let go: "What are you talking about? Come on, you're raving mad." It's not easy to provoke Aunt Quiz. She looks at him with a slightly mocking smile: "I see you don't grasp the concept, but it doesn't matter, Aunt Quiz will explain everything. Someday I might win a game show. The television people are sneaky, they might try to cheat me by offering a trip to Los Angeles as a prize. So I have to worry. If

I know in advance about the pedestrian crossings in Los Angeles, I'll be able to refuse and ask for an alternative. The Maldives or the Seychelles, for example, would suit me very well." No response from Giacomo.

I listen to the argument about Los Angeles with a cappuccino and a honey croissant. Today is an important day, historic, in fact. Appearing on the stage of the local news is a murderer, that is to say the Romanian Riina alias Deep Throat II. I pick up my newspaper and begin with the headline on the first page: THE ROMANIAN RIINA CONFESSES. Just underneath it is my name, along with Maritani's. The exposure continues. I read the first lines.

> Finally the murderer from the Romanian clan emerges from his silence. He calls himself Tigru, which means tiger in Romanian. He confesses to the murders of all the Albanians. Continued on p. 2.

Next to the main news story is a long editorial by the editor-in-chief, Salvini, with the title: OUR DEEP THROAT II. I read the beginning.

> After our exclusive account of the Albanian boss whom we dubbed Deep Throat I, our newspaper continues to investigate and, above all, to lay bare the background of the third Mafia war. Today we publish the confession of a prominent individual from the criminal world. It is our Deep Throat II, whom we'll call the Romanian Riina. His statements exonerate, at least in part, the young Romanian who was arrested, Adrian Nicolescu. We are undertaking a noble civic endeavor to reestablish the principles of justice. So we continue, with courage and intellectual honesty, to cast a sharp light on this terrible feud between Albanians and Romanians.

Blah blah blah. I don't have the patience to read the whole editorial, so I go to page two to check the confession of the Romanian Riina. I glance at it quickly; there aren't any changes or additions. It's the same version I gave Maritani yesterday. I scan the brief biographical profile of Toto Riina.

> Nicknamed 'u Curtu, because of his short stature, Riina was born in Corleone in 1930. He became head of the family at thirteen, after the death of his father in an accident, in which a younger brother also died. Along with Luciano Liggio and Bernardo Provenzano, he laid the foundations of the violent Corleonesi clan. At first his activity ranged from smuggling cigarettes to murder. Later he moved to drug trafficking. In 1969 he entered a long period of hiding. After the arrest of Liggio, in 1974, he became the uncontested boss of the Corleonesi. In the early eighties he ordered the killing of Stefano Bontate and Salvatore Inzerillo, two bosses of the Palermo Mafia. This marked the start of the Second Mafia War. Totò Riina, also known as the Beast, because of his ferocity, led the Corleonesi to final victory over Palermo.
>
> On January 15, 1993, he was captured in Palermo. He received multiple life sentences for murder. At present he is serving his term in the Opera prison in Milan.

The profile is exactly what I handed in to Maritani. I think the work came out well. I wait confidently for responses and especially congratulations. If I keep on with these scoops surely I'll win some prestigious prize.

After lunch Irene Morbidi comes to see me at the paper. She's really worried. Some of her more fanatical animal-rights companions want to take action before the pig is slaughtered or transformed by Mario Bellezza and company into a xenophobic and Fascist symbol. Gino a Fascist pig? I no longer understand anything about his various attributes: Italian, very Italian, Piedmontese, Turinese, Juventine, Po, and so on.

"Enzo, we have to find a solution right away, for Gino's good."

"I agree, but what can we do?"

"We're willing to take a step back."

"What is it?"

"We'll give up on the idea of having him."

"On condition that . . . "

"That he leaves the internment camp where he is now."

"Finally a step forward."

Irene is satisfied with the possible compromise. The story of Gino has provoked a lively discussion and has revived the core issues dear to the animal-rights advocates. Obviously some controversies remain. For example, how to make their voices heard? Is peaceful struggle effective or is strong action necessary? The important thing is for the animal-rights advocates of San Salvario to raise their voices in defense of animals. They are intensifying initiatives against hunting, and the city authorities will think more than twice before giving licenses to Muslims to open Islamic butcher shops. All thanks to Gino, the most famous piglet in San Salvario and vicinity.

"Enzo, the most practical solution is to take Gino to a park."

"A zoo?"

"No, for goodness' sake. Zoos are concentration camps for animals. There's a park near Turin where animals live happily and peacefully."

"Excellent idea. I'll talk to the others and let you know."

There are two secrets to being a good cook. First: the right cooking time, striking that delicate equilibrium between the raw and the cooked. Second: a harmonious balance of ingredients and spices. I make these expert-gastronome reflections as I'm tasting the famous *risotto alla Laganà*. The recipe isn't a secret, like Coca-Cola's, since many of my friends know it. Though I have to admit that I'm a little guarded with my recipes. I don't like to divulge them to everyone. Each is the product of experimentation, work, and time. Is it right to take advantage of the toil of others? Anyway, the *risotto alla Laganà* is made with brown rice. An important detail. And there is one indispensable ingredient: merguez, a fresh spicy sausage made with lamb, obviously *halal*, and popular among North Africans. I was able to perfect this recipe during my long stay in Marseilles when Jean-Pierre and I did our apartment swap.

Sara Bertini has arrived punctually. She looks beautiful, and is wearing a breathtaking décolleté. I greet her with two little kisses, the hell with a handshake. We sit in the living room and begin our evening with a good red Piedmontese wine, a Barbera.

"I like San Salvario a lot."

"It's nice. I haven't moved from here since I was born."

"So you're a genuine Piedmontese!"

"I? No, I'm a half-southerner, or rather a second-generation southerner. My parents came from Calabria."

We sit at the table. The risotto has a delicious aroma. I've also prepared a Calabrian antipasto. Obviously in this house there's no shortage of spiciness. The true Calabrian can't do without spice. Sara also likes spicy food, but for me it's essential. In the food department I'm faithful to my origins. As we eat, we talk about the transformation of Turin in recent years. The city of Fiat is disappearing; people don't buy cars the way they used to. Today the competition between car companies is ruthless, and things haven't gone well for Fiat; Turin is no longer a dream. Some lines of the Lucanian poet Rocco Scotellaro come to mind:

> Big-hearted Turin
> You're a girl, you take my hand

As I set out on the road:
They sent me far away,
Here, to people who dream of you as I do
In the wind of Fiats.

Today everyone agrees: Turin has to invent new models and aim at tourism and culture. A lot of money is being spent: where does it come from? And who is advancing it? If there are debts, as I suspect, who will pay them? San Salvario has changed a lot. Only a few years ago people were taking drugs on the street. The situation has improved immensely. When I talk about San Salvario, I become partisan. I'm profoundly in love with it. And, just like a lover, I don't see its flaws. For example, some people find the presence of prostitutes and transvestites on Via Nizza and Via Ormea an offense to decency. I, instead, believe that in San Salvario there is no social hypocrisy. We live in the light of the sun. We have everything, from the Madama Cristina market to the nearby station of Porta Nuova, from the beautiful Valentino park, open day and night, to the various churches, from the synagogue to the small Muslim prayer rooms, from the many restaurants that represent the kitchens of the world to the two historic porn cinemas on Via Principe Tommaso. Not to mention the inhabitants, who come from both the north and the south of Italy, and from all over the world.

I am a curious type by nature. I'm easily bored. I need to discover new things every day, otherwise I feel ill. How dull to live with a single language, with a single culture, a single cooking style. San Salvario is the supreme place of new discoveries. One thing for certain is that one will never die of boredom here. Sara is fascinated by my attachment to the neighborhood.

After the risotto we move to the balcony, which looks out on Via Galliari, to smoke.

"Enzo, can I ask you a question?"

"Of course."

"Did you really make that risotto?"

"Yes. Don't you believe me?"

"I believe you, and congratulate you. It was really wonderful."

"If you want I'll give you the recipe."

"Yes, thank you. Would you like a Marlboro?"

"No, thanks. I'm faithful to my MS."

Now comes an allusive message.

"I like men who are faithful."

The lovely Sara is playing along, which encourages me to continue.

"And why do you like faithful men?" I ask.

"Well, faithfulness is a sort of guarantee of love."

"But love is greater than faithfulness."

Love, faithfulness, blah blah blah. In other words, we're talking nonsense. Anyway, it's fine. Everything helps. The important thing is to heat up the mood a little.

When we start talking about "work," that is, the proposal to collaborate on a TV series, my enthusiasm diminishes.

Sara proposes that we watch the first episode of *The Octopus*. The one directed by Damiano Damiani, with Michele Placido in the role of Commissario Cattani. I agree—how can I refuse? For me, a film should be seen a single time and that's all. I find repeats really boring. But now the first episode of *Octopus* is starting. I hope I won't be compelled to watch the entire series. That would be torture. After ten minutes I move closer to her. I let a couple of scenes go by, I caress her hair, then her neck. She lets me. Solid encouragement to continue the expedition. I wait a few minutes before sending my pinkie to explore the two mountains. It's not difficult to get to the peak, the nipple emerges out of nothing. After a few seconds I hear her sighing. A volcano is waking up. I take her face in my hands, searching for her mouth. I tell *The Octopus* to get lost.

The light likewise. As I'm taking off her bra, I hear the doorbell. At first I pretend it's not happening, but the sound is continuous and deafening. I go to open the door and find myself facing Aunt Quiz in her nightgown.

"My TV isn't working. Can you come and take a look?"

"Tomorrow morning."

"No, tomorrow is too late. You have to come now. There's a quiz show starting."

"A quiz show at midnight?"

"Come on, let's not waste time."

"I'm coming."

God give me patience, as my mother would say. I go back to Sara to tell her about the Quiz emergency, she's standing up, and has already readjusted her shirt.

"Enzo, I have to go."

"Wait."

"We'll see each other again."

"Come on!"

Sara leaves under the amused gaze of my aunt. The piece of shit has ruined my evening and tomorrow morning early she will report everything to the big boss. There was nothing wrong with the TV, I just had to plug it in.

Chapter 11
A Quiz Can Save Your Life

Can one live in a freezer at fifty degrees below zero? Aunt Quiz swears it's possible. Where? In Yakutsk, in Siberia! There the inhabitants endure frigid cold. People die mostly in the spring, when the ice starts melting and chunks fall on the heads of passersby. Apparently, it's the leading cause of death. So my aunt warns me: don't ever go to Yakutsk between March and May, you could get killed! The great lesson is always the same: watching quiz shows is never a waste of time; it's a source of information and general culture. Quizzes can save you from various scams. For example, you win a quiz and the TV people, what do they do to reward you—they send you to die in Yakutsk. A quiz can save your life. Forewarned is forearmed.

The cold of Yakutsk leads us automatically to talk of the high cost of heat in San Salvario and in Turin in general. My aunt doesn't miss the chance to complain about the managers of the building, a gang of greedy crooks. What's the use of heat if people in Yakutsk live at peace with the cold? Obviously there's no shortage of scoundrels: doctors and pharmacists. Why? First of all, they make a living off of cold and exploit the winter to make money. They're the ones who spread the flu virus and then provide worthless vaccines!

I listen to Aunt Quiz's outburst as I'm going up the stairs to Joseph's, to try and resolve the damn business of the piglet. Now I have a specific proposal, from Amin & brothers, to waive consignment of the pig. I hope my Nigerian friend will agree. It's the last resort. If he refuses I give up. I throw in the sponge. I can't do any more. Joseph opens the door with the usual precautions. I find him tired and stressed. He says that the owner of the apartment, who lives in Venice, called to ask for an explanation. Someone in San Salvario informed on him. Now he's at risk of being unable to renew his lease. That is a huge problem, it would delay the whole matter of the family reunion. How will he welcome his wife and children, who are arriving soon? But I tell him about the new developments. He listens carefully. I don't know how long he can continue to hold out in this condition, hounded in his own apartment.

"Joseph, you can't go on like this."

"You're right."

"Now you have to choose between the pig and your family."

"A difficult choice."

"It's time for you to make a compromise, too," I urge him.

"What should I do, Enzo?"

"Give up the pig."

"I accept that, but I want a guarantee for Gino's future."

"Guarantee?"

"I mean, that he won't be killed."

"As for that, I can guarantee it myself. He'll go to a beautiful park for animals."

"Enzo, the important thing is for Gino to emerge from this business with his head held high."

"Don't worry. Gino will never be defeated."

Gino's future! The important thing is for Gino to emerge from this business with his head held high! Now Joseph is verging on madness. His delirium has no bounds. In the end we come to an agreement on some practical matters. I will be the one to take the pig and transport him to the park, since Joseph doesn't trust anyone else. And Joseph will be able to visit his beloved Gino whenever he wants.

If we want to arrest criminals we should return to the great lessons of the Westerns and follow the practice of putting a price on their heads, with the famous *Wanted! Dead or Alive* posters. One colleague points out that in the United States the profession of bounty hunter still exists. Certainly there are no longer cowboys on horseback; they use other means, like ships, helicopters, or very well-equipped cars. Another recalls that there's an American TV series about a former cop who becomes a bounty hunter.

Yet another colleague, I would say somewhat nostalgic, maintains that to defeat crime we have to use strong-arm tactics and implement two measures. First: bring back the death penalty, abolished in Italy in 1948. Second: follow the Saudi and Iranian model and carry out hangings in the public squares.

I am present, very bored, at this chat during the editorial meeting. I might as well be in Giacomo's bar. What should we do? Luckily the meeting doesn't last long. Maritani asks me to stay; he wants to talk to me privately about something important.

"News from our Deep Throats I and II?"

Nothing," I answer.

"It's strange. The feud between the Albanians and the Romanians stopped suddenly. Why? What happened, in your opinion?"

"I don't know."

Maritani slowly comes out into the open. He talks about internal and external pressures, from phone calls from the editor-in-chief Salvini at the head office to pleas from the paper's most important shareholders. They're all asking to keep the story going. Obviously there's been a revival of the self-important, envious rumors, claiming that the third Mafia war is only an invention, a big hoax, as they say. And what does this mean? That the Albanian Buscetta and the Romanian Riina never existed, they're merely figments? For my editor, Mafia wars do not end like this. The body count is higher; there's more blood, more damage, more outrage. There must be some reason. We've got to get in touch with our Deep Throats immediately to find out what's happening.

I promise Maritani that I'll get busy right away.

I go to my office to reflect seriously on this problem. I start with a basic question: how do wars end? When there is a winner and a loser. Or when an agreement is reached, a peace treaty. And there are no treaties without mediation! Here's what it takes to explain why the supposed feud between the Albanians and Romanians unexpectedly broke off. A really crazy idea starts buzzing in my ear. I have to talk to Luciano Terni.

Between one thing and another I don't ignore my physical and mental well-being. I call Sara Bertini for the hundredth time on her cell phone, but she's unavailable. What a pity! I was very close to the source of my well-being. It's useless to cry over spilled milk. I'm confident. As long as there's the non-E.U. *Octopus* there's hope.

On the way home, I run into Aunt Quiz. She's always good-humored and, above all, energetic. I don't know where she gets all that strength. Somewhere she must have a magic substance, an elixir. The ills of society are often attributed to TV, but it has to be said that auntie uses TV to be informed, entertained, and to obtain a good general education. If I'm not mistaken those are the very objectives of the BBC, the best model for TV there is. Wouldn't it be a good idea to entrust our public television to Aunt Quiz?

"Enzo, it can't go on like this."

"What happened, auntie?"

"You have to intervene immediately to resolve the pig problem."

"We're trying."

My aunt explains her fears. In this affair there's a complete lack of common sense. All sides think they can end it by force. The men in the mosque aren't joking; after the attacks on the Twin Towers the world shouldn't underestimate their threats. Oh, the Twin Towers, my aunt dreamed of winning a quiz and getting to go and visit them. Too bad, she'll never be able to. The Muslims have no sense of irony or self-mockery, and they're easily offended. A few simple caricatures were enough to provoke their rage. The members of the Masters in Our Own House committee, Mario Bellezza at the top of the list, are rather childish, they confuse politics with religion, animals with traditions, a piglet with a crucifix. Not to mention the Nigerian. For at least eighty years, that is, since Aunt Quiz set foot in this world, nobody has raised a pig in an apartment around here. He's either crazy or retarded. There is no third explanation. Her criticism doesn't spare even Irene and her association for the defense of animals. In the end, treating animals with humanity and mercy is a good thing, but to consider them human beings is pure childishness.

With incredible lucidity she presents her opinion on how to resolve the problem. First of all, some crucial details need to be analyzed. For example, finding out who was behind that wicked deed doesn't matter, so there's no point in trying to establish the guilt or innocence of the African and his pig. Right now, it's more important to defuse this bomb before it explodes. The bomb is the pig, and therefore he has to be moved somewhere, at least temporarily.

Auntie is up on all the details. She knows about my negotiations and is familiar with the various positions. She has first-rate sources. On one point she is perfectly right: there needs to be an intervention, and soon. Finally my aunt reveals a small secret.

"Enzo, I'm on the right track."

"What track, auntie?"

"An investigative path that will yield the name and last name of the culprit in the affair of the pig."

"What have you discovered?"

"I have good evidence."

"Can you tell me anything in advance?" I ask.

"Not now—when I have proof."

"All right."

To bring my delicate mediation to an end I decide not to exclude any party. It's an intelligent way of avoiding complications in forging a solution. Gino will go to a park for animals. No one will feel defeated. I meet Mario Bellezza at the committee headquarters, in Via Baretti. I tell him about the proposal for a definitive resolution of the business of the pig. He interrupts me frequently to ask questions. I don't know if he does it from a need to understand or for the pleasure of annoying me.

"We want guarantees, Enzo."

"Such as?"

"The Muslims have to stay away from the Piedmontese pig."

"As I told you, he'll go to a park near Turin."

"So still in Padania?"

"Exactly."

For Bellezza, this proposal is more than reasonable. He promises me a quick response after the Masters in Our Own House committee meets, tonight. But it's a pure formality. He's in charge: the other members are merely extras. Finally I begin to see a ray of light. Hooray!

In order not to waste time, I go directly to the mosque on Via Galliari. Amin welcomes me to a small room that functions as an office.

"Dear Amin, we have a solution."

"*Allahu Akbar*, God is great!"

The idea of taking the pig to a park gets Amin's full consent.

He's a smart guy. He knows that it's risky for the mosque to be too much in the spotlight. The local authorities could close it at any moment. It's very easy to invent a pretext. They'd only have to send the police to inspect and declare the place unfit because it doesn't meet the standards of safety and hygiene. Of course, if those criteria were applied to the public schools in Italy, more than half of them would be closed.

Amin has carte blanche to make a decision in this case and that simplifies my task. For him, the main goal is to get the pig out of San Salvario and end the controversies among the mosque faithful. Coming together again as a united front is a priority in view of future battles to obtain a real place of worship. The prophet Mohammed warned Muslims against divisiveness. There is always strength in unity. For my part, I try to get some guarantees on Joseph's future. Amin is clear: "For us, the business will be finished. No revenge, you have our word. Islam is also a religion of forgiveness."

That evening I find Luciano Terni in a small theater near Porta Palazzo. He's rehearsing a new show, a theatrical adaptation of Luigi Zampa's film *A Girl in Australia*, with the great Alberto Sordi. Luciano is constantly experimenting, bringing Italian comedy from the movies to the theater. Two years ago he did a terrific show based on Mario Monicelli's *We Want the Colonels*, where he was the main character, played in the film by Ugo Tognazzi.

"Dear Enzo, you have the shit-eating grin you always have when you're in trouble."

"Let's not exaggerate, I just have a small problem."

"And obviously you need me."

"Exactly. At the paper they're starting to doubt the Albanian Buscetta and the Romanian Riina."

"What's the matter? Wasn't the performance of the Romanian Riina good?"

"No, absolutely, the performance was perfect. The problem is that they're wondering why there aren't any more murders."

"They're not wrong. Mafia wars are always bloody and long," Luciano reasons.

"So we have to find an explanation. We could say, for instance, that the feud ended because there were negotiations, a truce, an agreement."

"What are you thinking of, Enzo?"

"I have in mind a new character, a sort of peacemaker or mediator."

"Give me the script."

"This one's hard. I don't know if you'd feel like doing it."

"The true artist challenges the whole world, including himself."

"I agree."

Perfect. I've touched the highest point of his vanity, his artistic pride. I explain to Luciano that Deep Throat III will be a woman, a Nigerian *maman*, a madam, and that, as is often the case, she's also a retired prostitute. Her role is to "educate" and prepare young girls for the world's oldest profession. Our *maman* is around forty, with a booming, slightly masculine voice. She's lived in Italy for twenty years. After working as a prostitute she has set up a small ring, exploiting a dozen girls from her country. Deep Throat III has been directed by the criminal organizations to put an end to the Albanian-Romanian feud. Why was she chosen? A basic question. The main thing is that she's impartial, as she's a woman, black, African, and animist, while the Albanians and the Romanians are men, white, and European, the only difference between them being that the former are Muslim and the latter Christian.

Luciano is really enthusiastic. He immediately begins to think about the character. Inspiration in art is essential. A couple of films come to mind: *Tootsie*, with Dustin Hoffman playing a young, difficult actor; and *La Cage aux Folles*, with the great Ugo

Tognazzi, his favorite actor. We quickly arrange the other details of the interview, like the time and the compensation.

"Have you heard about this business of the piglet in San Salvario?" Luciano asks me.

"Of course. It took place in my building."

"Really?"

"Plus I'm one of the main players."

I tell Luciano the behind-the-scenes story of Gino. He asks a lot of questions to satisfy his curiosity. Every so often he makes a note in his notebook, from which he is inseparable.

"Enzo, you remember *The Caucasian Chalk Circle*?"

"No."

"It's a play by Brecht."

"And what does it have to do with the pig of San Salvario?"

It has a lot to do with it. A governor's wife abandons her son during a revolt that leads to the killing of the governor. The baby is saved by a scullery maid, a peasant woman who nurses him. Years pass, the mother reappears and wants her child. But the adoptive mother won't agree. The fight reaches a judge, who finds an effective solution: he draws a chalk circle and puts the contested child in the center. The two mothers have to pull him, from opposite sides. Whoever wins the duel will be awarded the child. The peasant woman yields, in order not to hurt the child. This is enough for the judge to come to a decision and give her the child. Without forcing the metaphor too much, the piglet Gino is the contested prince.

"Enzo, the story of Gino could become a fine reworking of Brecht's play."

"Do you have a title in mind?"

"*Dispute Over an Italian Piglet in San Salvario*. What do you say?

"I like it, but I'd say "'Very Italian' instead of 'Italian.'" I pile it on.

Chapter 12
God Bless Negotiations

I wake up suddenly, frightened. Someone is pressing the doorbell incessantly, and I hear loud shouts. What's happening? A fire? An earthquake? A murder? I open the door, and there is Aunt Quiz, very agitated.

"They've come to kidnap the pig."

"Who?"

"The neighborhood police."

"Where's Joseph?"

"He's barricaded inside and won't open the door. They're about to call in reinforcements. Come right now and reason with him."

"I'm coming."

I pull on jeans and a T-shirt and run up to the third floor. To see so many cops, ready to intervene, makes a certain impression. I remember the sad end, two years ago, of Latifa Sdairi, a nineteen-year-old Moroccan girl who died jumping from the roof of the building where she lived, at Via Berthollet 8. She wanted to escape from the police. She was afraid of being expelled, because she didn't have a residency permit. A life cut off for an absurd reason.

The head of the San Salvario local police, Damiano Pazzini, is an old acquaintance. I've interviewed him many times, and as soon as he sees me he gives me a smile. The others follow the example of their chief. It seems I'm becoming a celebrity, at least in the neighborhood of San Salvario. Pazzini explains the situation. It's very delicate. It will take common sense and collaboration, and we have to act with caution to avoid the worst. It's in everyone's interest to resolve the matter peacefully—the use of force should be a last option. The piglet has to be seized on the basis of the article in the penal code on the mistreatment of animals. He takes a sheet of paper out of his pocket and starts reading: "Article 544-c. Anyone who, cruelly or unnecessarily, causes harm to an animal or subjects him to maltreatment or to behavior or labors or tasks unsuitable for his ethological characteristics is to be punished with imprisonment for three months to a year or a fine of 3,000 to 15,000 euros."

The law is clear and must be obeyed. This is a point that cannot be ignored. Joseph listens from behind the door and he won't accept it. He's enraged: "Me, reported for mistreatment of animals? Are you crazy? I've never mistreated Gino, I've always protected him. I risked my life for him. You should arrest the people who want to kill him." Pazzini proves to be diplomatic, and promises that the piglet will be taken to a suitable institution. My Nigerian friend keeps trying to get guarantees for Gino's future (still this business of the future). He asks him to clarify what "suitable institution" means. A slaughterhouse might also be considered a suitable institution. The expression is vague, it means everything and nothing. On this point he's certainly not wrong.

I interrupt to explain and, above all, to pacify. Aunt Quiz, too, helps with soothing words. This old lady has so many resources—she never ceases to amaze me. Anyway, after a long and exhausting back-and-forth, Joseph avoids the worst, that is arrest, and agrees to give up Gino. The cops carry off the pig with the Juventus scarf. The final insult to the team and its fans. One defeat after another. Hell, wasn't it enough to send us down to Series B?

Joseph, however, is unyielding, he intends to go on a hunger strike and find a lawyer. He's ready to fight to the end to defend his dignity. He doesn't want to be seen as a torturer of animals. He loved Gino. How will he endure this painful separation? What can we do? We'll stay close to him.

Before going to the office to see Maritani I light an MS to release a little tension. I'll have to concentrate now to avoid anything unexpected. The big celebration for the arrival of Deep Throat III is about to begin. Entertainment is guaranteed. Act I: I go to Maritani. Act II: I repeat the same nonsense as for Deep Throat I and II. Third and final act: Maritani the editor, Salvini, the editor-in-chief, and the national and international public get it in the rear. End of the show. Isn't it great?

"Angelo, I discovered why the feud between the Albanians and the Romanians stopped."

"Really? I'm all ears."

"Negotiations are under way."

"My intuition was right."

"You were perfectly correct," I confirm.

"What did you find?"

"I've unearthed the mediator who's leading the negotiations."

"You're not telling me we have Deep Throat III?"

"Exactly that."

"Hooray! We need to update the results of the match, immediately," Maritani says exultantly.

"Washington *Post* 1–our newspaper 3."

"Bravo. Who is this mediator?"

"A woman, a former Nigerian prostitute."

"A woman! Who gave her the job? The Italian state?"

"No."

"The Cosa Nostra?"

"No."

"The'ndragheta?"

"No."

"The Casalesi?"

"No."

"Then who?"

"The Nigerian mafia."

"That's a real surprise."

"A big surprise," I agree.

Like hell a big surprise! Maritani, euphoric, calls Salvini to update him. Obviously he's going to milk this for all it's worth. Suddenly he's an expert on the subject, a sort of mafiologist. According to him, the Nigerian mafia now rules the criminal world here. Why? For the simple reason that no one can be a peacemaker or mediator without possessing power, charisma, and authority. And also because agreements require powers of persuasion and, when necessary, coercion. It's not easy to get criminal gangs to respect an agreement. I prefer not to add anything, Maritani is enough and more. I confine myself to accepting Salvini's congratulations, and I thank him.

Before I go, we take a moment to settle the details of the interview with Deep Throat III. We could set up an agency devoted exclusively to this. Nothing changes with respect to the two preceding ones: same place, same method, same time, same compensation.

At lunchtime Inspector Contini comes to see me at the paper. He's smiling. But I don't trust his smile. I invite him into my little office. I hope he doesn't waste my time and above all that he doesn't make me blow my cool.

"I wouldn't like to be in your position, Laganà."

"Why, inspector?"

"Suspicions are increasing. The supposed feud between Albanians and Romanians has come to nothing."

"I just do my work as a reporter, no more, no less."

"Behind the homicides is the 'ndrangheta, dear Laganà. I even know the name of the mastermind."

"Who is it?"

"Don't be naïve, Laganà. You know what I think?"

"Tell me, inspector."

According to him, the possibilities are two: either I've been tricked by someone or I'm an accomplice. A feud between Albanians and Romanians never existed. The foreign criminals, especially the Albanians and the Romanians, are settling smoothly into the Italian criminal world. In his view I will not emerge from this story unharmed. I'll be sacked from the newspaper and banned from the fraternity of journalists. What Contini has not yet understood is this: I can't be blackmailed. I'm not afraid. I feel free. I don't have great responsibilities. I don't have a family to support, my mother doesn't depend on me financially. And I don't have a mortgage to pay off. As for being an accomplice, there's only my Calabrian origins. The theory is simple: all Calabrians are 'ndranghetisti. But it's not easy to prove.

"All you have are suspicions and hypotheses, inspector."

"The proof will emerge. You might as well come clean now."

"Thank you for the advice."

Contini really feels a profound hatred toward me, and he won't miss an opportunity to screw me. So I had better be careful, the road is a minefield. I say nothing to the inspector about the arrival of the Nigerian woman, our Deep Throat III. I like to surprise. I'd really like to see his reaction when he reads this new testimony in the newspaper.

Here we are for the third time, in the same uninhabited apartment. Except that Maritani has forgotten the thermos of coffee. I'm a little worried and tense. Luciano Terni is a real genius at imitation, but the new enterprise is tough. Imitating a female voice is no joke, no walk in the Valentino. The phone rings. I push the green button and put it on speaker.

"Hello, ma'am, it's Laganà. As we agreed, I'm with my editor, Maritani."

"Hello, Mr. Laganà. Dear Maritani, how are you?"

"Fine, ma'am."

"Maritani, excuse me if I address you with the informal *tu*. I somehow can't be formal with you."

"That's no problem, ma'am."

"Thank you. May I ask you a question?"

"Of course."

"Why don't you go on TV like the editor-in-chief, Salvini?"

"Because I haven't been asked."

"Then you'd better get busy. Remember, if you're not on TV you're nothing, less than shit. Excuse the swear word."

"It's true. How would you like us to address you?"

"Call me Madame."

"Perfect. Madame, our readers would like to know you."

"I'm ready."

The interview proceeds without blunders or exaggerations. Luciano's performance is truly magnificent, utterly convincing. Afterward, Maritani gives me the same assignment as the other times: transcribing the interview in the form of a first-person account makes it more immediate, more engaging to the reader.

On the way home I get an SMS. "Dear Laganà, there is a gift for you at Giacomo's bar. Follow the file. Happy reading. See you soon. Very Deep Throat." Same unknown origin as the others. Now I have no reason to doubt its credibility. So far, the mysterious source alias Very Deep Throat hasn't misled me.

I stop at Giacomo's. I usually come by in the morning. As soon as he sees me he says there's a package for me. It was delivered a short time ago by a messenger. There are no other details, so it can't be traced back to the sender. I sit down and open it. I find photocopies of invoices, documents, photographs, newspaper clippings. I immediately understand the importance of the material, and decide to go home.

I like to read lying on my bed, where there's plenty of space to organize the papers. Of course it's not comfortable for writing, but for taking notes it's fine. I start with the invoices: they're all photocopied and bear the letterhead of the Belpaese real-estate consortium, our paper's biggest advertiser.

I'm stunned as I read the board members: it's the *crème de la crème*, former ministers, former generals, bankers, famous journalists . . .

I glance at the eight photographs, which were taken secretly. Five people are sitting around a table, having lunch or dinner, in a spirit of conviviality. They're all laughing. I'm able to recognize two faces: Paolo Manzoni, a well-known politician, and Antonino Scaliani, the head of a branch of the Petri clan. On the back of one of the photos are names: I was right about the first two, the others are Bertini cousins, members of the board of Belpaese. Sara Bertini! She can't have been sent by her family to spy on me? Why did she appear and disappear so suddenly? And what happened to her project, the *Octopus* featuring non-E.U. citizens?

It takes a couple of hours to read all the documents. There are things I already know about the 'ndrangheta. For example, the *locale* is the basic territorial structure that allows one or more *'ndrina*, or clan, to organize its own criminal activities. Every *'ndrina* is based on blood ties, and so there are very few collaborators with the law in the 'ndrangheta, unlike the Camorra and Cosa Nostra, even though its strategy has changed, and there's a new type of member, called the "made man," who is not of Calabrian origin. It's well known that the 'ndrangheta originated in a context of poverty. Maybe at the beginning it was like that, but later, with drug trafficking and kidnappings, huge sums of money accumulated. The 'ndrangheta never has liquidity problems. It's stronger than any bank—a crime syndicate with branches all over the world. That's a more up-to-date description.

Finally, there are two fundamental things that shouldn't be forgotten. First, the 'ndrangheta carries out the same function as other criminal organizations, that is, it fills the void left by the state. Second, without politics and without an economy, organized crime would not exist.

While I'm making myself some pasta I get a strange telephone call from my old acquaintance Franco Tamburo, the baronet of thieves and fences. He urges me to be careful, someone is planning to steal something from me. He remembered the favor, or, rather, the pseudo favor, of Taina's suitcase, passed off as a suitcase belonging to the Security Services.

"What is supposed to be stolen from me?" I ask.

"I don't know."

"Who are the thieves?" I insist.

"It doesn't matter who they are. Keep an eye on your things."

"Why this message in code?"

"I can't tell you more, Enzo. I'm sorry."

"You have to keep your professional secrets."

"That's right."

"Thanks for the tip, Franco."

I decide not to go out tonight, I'll do like Joseph. I have to keep an eye on the loot. I don't know what to do. I realize the significance of the documents. I have a scoop on my hands, in fact a bomb. Tomorrow I'll figure something out: I can't leave a ticking bomb here; it needs a safer place. I have to talk to Maritani, we'll see if they've got the balls to publish this stuff. I'll try it, but I won't make too big a fuss. This job has taught me that when the game gets rough not everybody wants to play. It's much better to stay on the sidelines or in the stands and watch. To forget about all this, I try to relax, listening to the rebel Rino Gaetano, a southerner like me. I start with a good song:

> But the sky is always bluer uh-uh-uh-er,
> Who dreams of millions, who gambles,
> Who plays with string, who's turned a deaf ear
> Who is a farmer, who sweeps the courtyards.

Chapter 13
The Fish Is Good, But It Has Bones

I'm called Madame, and I was born in Benin City, in southern Nigeria. When I was a child I was called Beauty because I was very pretty. But beautiful things don't last, unfortunately.

We have a proverb that goes: *The fish is good, but it has bones*. Just like life. One of those bones is my father, who abandoned us to go and live with his fourth wife, a very cruel woman. My mother worked as a seamstress, and she couldn't support six children by herself. I was the oldest, so I had to think of some way to help the family. At sixteen I took the advice of my cousin who lived in Italy. I still remember her wretched words: "Beauty, you're a pretty girl, in a short time you could earn a lot of money with your body. It would be really too bad for someone like you to spend your life in poverty!" I accepted her offer, convincing myself that even if "selling my body" was a bad job, it was no different from plenty of other kinds of commerce. My priority was to save my younger siblings from poverty. The rest didn't much matter.

It was my cousin's husband who arranged everything and paid the expenses of the trip. He told me to be calm and not to worry, there would be plenty of time to pay back the money. The day before my departure he took me to Babaloa to perform a voodoo rite: I walked on my knees for half an hour, then with my bare hands I killed a chicken. I had to gut it with a knife and eat the raw heart. I couldn't do it and I kept vomiting. In the end I swore to obey my cousin: I didn't know she would be my *maman*, that is my pimp. If I disobeyed, the punishment would be very harsh: my mother would be burned to death or one of my siblings would be maimed for life. I believe in voodoo, so I never rebelled, by going to the police and telling them everything.

The trip to Italy lasted ten days. There were five of us, four girls and our chaperon or jailer. First we went to Dakar, then to Casablanca. From there we took a plane to Rome, then the train to Turin, where my cousin was waiting for us.

My first encounter with Turin is still vivid. The same day my cousin told me that I owed a debt of sixty million lire, that is around thirty thousand euros! A real trap. A rope around my neck. The next day she taught me a few phrases in Italian that would be useful in my new profession: ten thousand lire for a blow job, twenty thousand lire with a condom, thirty thousand without a condom, fifty thousand for the ass.

I remember the first night. I was alone on a dark street; it was very cold and pouring rain. I was terrified, I wept and prayed in silence. The cars didn't stop and it seemed as if the time would never pass. I hadn't ever imagined having sex in a car. I thought the Italians were rich, that they could afford at least a room in a small hotel. I thought I would be a prostitute in a night club or discotheque, warm and safe, with men who were handsome, elegant, refined, generous, and, above all, rich, men who would cover me with jewels and valuable gifts. Instead I ended up on the meanest streets, without pity, forgotten even by God. My clients were poor working men, young unemployed men, lowlife immigrants, and maniacs of all types, in other words cruel and desperate people.

Anyway, as time goes on you get used to everything, even if the fear never really faded. I was afraid of getting seriously ill, like so many of my friends who died of AIDS. Fortunately that didn't happen to me, because I almost always worked with a condom. But sometimes I also did without, especially when it was a bad night, and there weren't many cars, I mean not many clients. Then I agreed to anything. I couldn't go home with empty pockets. I got pregnant only once, I had to go to a Chinese woman in Rome for an illegal abortion. I paid a good three million lire. A real disaster.

After years of work on the street nothing remained of my beauty, except the name. Beauty is a flower that needs to be carefully tended. I didn't have time to think of my body the way all women do; I had other priorities. I was like the song by Loredana Bertè, my favorite singer:

> I'm not a lady
> I'm a woman whose war is never over
> I'm not a lady
> A woman with too many marks in life
> Oh no, oh no

Now, however, I am a true lady and so I am called Madame.

But let's get to this terrible white-European feud. When I started as a prostitute, there was a lot of work for the Nigerians. In the late nineties the Albanians and girls from the East arrived, and they ruined the market for us. They were young, pretty, and white, and so the Italian clients liked them. Also, they had extremely violent Albanian pimps. Slowly they pushed us out of our spots, those squalid stretches of sidewalk where girls wait for clients. You paid a monthly fee of a hundred and fifty to three hundred euros. When I realized that there wouldn't be much work for me, because of my age and the competition with the girls from the East, I began work as a *maman*. I invested my savings in a project: I paid to bring over a lot of pretty young girls from Benin City. At the moment I have thirty. I put at their disposal my long experience. The Albanian and Romanian pimps—all they know is violence. We instead have voodoo. There's no need to beat disobedient girls.

I've often tried to persuade my colleagues from Eastern Europe to adopt voodoo, offering free courses, but they always refuse. They say, "Voodoo is primitive and isn't part of our tradition. We are Europeans." A stupid answer. I've also suggested the creation of a sort of national union of pimps to defend the interests of the profession, but without results. I've often protested against the unfair competition of their girls, who earn twice as much as mine. It's not right. Do we offer the same services or not? It's racism. Anyway, the present feud is the consequence of mistaken methods, because violence can't resolve all problems.

Many may wonder why I was chosen to be the mediator. Well, the answer is simple. I am unprejudiced: I'm a woman, black, African, and animist, whereas they are male, white, European, and monotheistic. If I may, I'd like to say, no offense, that we women are more intelligent. Men are stupid because they love violence.

The negotiations are very complex, but we're at a good point. The truce is proceeding well. I did a lot of work to put an end to this terrible feud. If I succeed in this mission, I'd like to be a candidate for the Nobel Peace Prize. I'd ask everyone to support me.

Last Chapter
One Who Is Afraid Dies Every Day

I put the file from Very Deep Throat in my backpack and go to the café for breakfast. I stop at the newsstand to get the papers. Today is christening day for Deep Throat III. I sit down and begin with the headline on the first page: THE THIRD MAFIA WAR IS OVER. A subhead follows: MEDIATOR TALKS ABOUT NEGOTIATIONS. Underneath, Maritani's name and mine. I read the beginning:

> The public has recently been wondering why there have been no more murders in the bloody Albanian-Romanian feud. Today our paper is able to provide the answer. Testimony from the Nigerian mediator who is in charge of negotiations between the clans is published today exclusively in this paper. Continued on page 2.

Let's see the rest. There's a photograph of African women in bright-colored clothes, probably taken at the market in Porta Palazzo. A photograph of Deep Throat III, alias Madame, is not yet available. I glance quickly at the story. It's identical to what I wrote and delivered yesterday to Maritani. Next to the testimony are a couple of sidebars, the first on Nigeria, the second on Nigerian immigrants in Italy. The figures are reliable; they're taken from the annual statistics compiled by Caritas. I return to the first page. The editorial of our editor-in-chief Salvini awaits me.

I have always maintained that a newspaper can't live without the support and affection of its readers. We are always at your service, dear readers. We have followed the third Mafia war from the start, we have disclosed all, warning citizens and the authorities. Today we are happy to announce three very important news items. First: we have our Deep Throat III. Second: very delicate negotiations to put an end to a terrible chain of homicides in Turin are about to conclude, successfully we hope. Third: leading these negotiations is a Nigerian immigrant woman. As that visionary poet Louis Aragon saw clearly: "Women are the future of men."

What a toady this Salvini is. Who knows if he'll have the chance to repeat these gems on *Rear Window* in the next few days. The phone rings.

"Listen: I've decided to come back and live in Turin."

"What? Who's going to take care of grandma?"

"It's not a problem. I can find an immigrant caretaker or bring her with me to Turin."

"It doesn't seem like a good idea, Mamma."

"My place is in Turin, not here in Cosenza."

"What do you have to do here?"

"There's a lot of work. For example I could look after that wretched son of mine who is always getting in trouble."

"Come on, Mamma! Do we have to fight now?"

The real reason for my mother's rage is the publication of the story of Deep Throat III. I let her vent for twenty minutes or so. She repeats the usual nonsense: I'm on the threshold of forty, I have no wife or children, and, above all, I don't own a house. Obviously she doesn't forget to cite at least twice cousin Pietro, the boy father of twins. She asks a few questions about Joseph and his piglet. She is very well informed. Her source is first-rate. Finally she calms down a bit and decides to put off the decision to come and live with me in San Salvario. Of course: it's only a reprieve.

"Listen, I almost forgot. I asked Natalia if starting tomorrow she can take care of all the bills."

"Why?"

"Because you're always in a daze. Did you pay the last gas bill?"

"No, I don't think so."

"You see? It was due the day before yesterday."

"Yes, ma'am!"

I don't know how to deal with her. I don't like to make her angry, but sometimes she drives me crazy. My mother has a third cousin who operates a newsstand here in Turin. It's her press office. Whenever an article of mine comes out the shit calls right away and tells her.

Leaving the bar I run into spy No. 1, alias Aunt Quiz. She takes me aside to tell me something confidential.

"I've finally got the proof. I've discovered the culprit."

"What are you talking about, auntie?"

"The business of the pig. Promise you'll keep the secret?"

"I promise."

The person who staged the pig's walk through the mosque was Giorgio, the twelve-year-old son of the Tardinis, who live right above Joseph. A couple of friends helped him. The motive was apparently neither religious nor political. He had made a bet with some schoolmates without thinking too hard about the consequences. It might have been a test to be admitted to the group. In other words, kids' stuff.

Aunt Quiz tells me that the Tardinis are nice people. They're really sorry, and they want to apologize to Joseph and to the heads of the mosque. I offer to get everyone together and end, once and for all, the controversies over Gino the piglet.

At the office I run into some of my colleagues, who congratulate me on the scoop of Deep Throat III. I go to Maritani's office. I notice a major change. The Padre Pio calendar is no longer hanging next to the poster of *All the President's Men*. It's been replaced by today's front page. Reading the main headline and the subhead up on the wall makes an impression.

"Salvini is very pleased. Tonight he'll be back on TV, on *Rear Window*."

"Fantastic."

"Dear Enzo, we are writing a glorious page in Italian and perhaps world journalism. Our case will set a trend."

"I'm glad."

What can I say? Would it be right to break the spell? By now he's hopeless. The problem is, I'm very allergic to excitement, it gives me heart trouble. Maritani strains my nerves. He tells me that we have to aim higher. Now that this story of the Albanians-Romanians feud is over, the two of us have to get busy and write a good book, like Woodward and Bernstein. It will become a successful film. On this point he has no doubts. Famous actors will play our characters. In his role he sees someone like Robert De Niro. In mine Alessandro Gassmann will be good, with his Mediterranean face. Of course, he's not his father, but he's very good.

"I already have in mind a terrific title for our book."

"What is it?"

"*Deep Throats. An Italian Story*. Isn't it good?"

"Very good."

Maritani insists: we have to move in a hurry, there's a publisher interested. Maybe we can get it out in a few months. This is the right moment. We have to strike while the iron is hot, all too soon people will be talking about something else. This is our profession, it's not a secret. The book won't require too much effort and time, we just have to write an introduction and a conclusion, and obviously organize the material, the various interviews with our deep throats and the different reactions to the case.

A book about the Deep Throats with my name on the cover? Not a chance. Let's move on to more serious matters.

"Angelo, I'd like to talk to you about a different scoop."

"Don't tell me we have Deep Throat IV?"

"We have Very Deep Throat."

I start with an introduction about the mysterious source in order to get his careful attention. Then I pull the file out of my backpack. I show Maritani the photographs and the invoices and other documents. I give a concise summary of the material. He listens closely. At the end he reacts like a disciplined soldier and, with his great respect for hierarchy, calls Salvini. He reports faithfully. After a few minutes he hangs up and looks at me with an indecipherable smile.

"The editor-in-chief says we should let it go."

"Why?"

The Belpaese consortium is our biggest advertiser. Also, Turin doesn't need bad publicity, especially after the great success of the Winter Olympics. We mustn't be spoilsports and damage the image of a beautiful new city. In other words, it's better not to talk about the Mafia, the 'ndrangheta, the Camorra of the north, otherwise money and tourists will go elsewhere.

"Enzo, I almost forgot. I'd like to talk to you about something else."

"Yes?"

"We have to do something on the piglet in San Salvario."

"What?"

Maritani shows me a news bulletin that recounts the seizure of the piglet. It would be great to do the story. Give the background, anecdotes, the various characters, and so on. In short, a light, amusing article. It would be an effective way of brightening up the atmosphere after the business of the feud. I decline the offer diplomatically. It's better to entrust the job to some colleague, I can't be objective, I'm too involved. An SMS arrives: "Dear Laganà, Be in the Valentino in two hours, at the entrance to the architecture school. Come alone. Very Deep Throat." Without hesitation I decide to go to the appointment. I'm not going to miss the chance to meet my mysterious source in person.

The Valentino is full of memories for me, more than any other place. A tide of memories from childhood and adolescence rise before me. Here I am playing with my sister Paola (under Mamma's strict supervision) or kicking a ball while my father pretends to block it. Here I am lying under a tree, exchanging brief kisses, or hanging out nights amid bottles of beer and joints. Abruptly the memories are interrupted. I hear footsteps behind me, and I turn suddenly.

"Hi, Enzo."

"Sara!"

"Very Deep Throat, to be exact."

"Did your father send you to spy on me?"

"Unfortunately, poor Papa doesn't count for anything anymore."

"Then what game are you playing? And what happened to our *Octopus*?"

"It was only a hook."

"Congratulations."

"I didn't want to deceive you, Enzo. It was the only way of approaching without rousing suspicions."

"Now explain this mess."

We go into the park and sit on a bench. Sara lights a Marlboro and makes a short introduction: she investigated thoroughly before approaching me. Finally she reached the conclusion that I am a respectable, reliable person.

The story begins long ago. After the Second World War

Sara's grandfather, a young, ambitious, and enterprising bricklayer, founds a small construction company in Turin. Gradually it becomes a large presence throughout Piedmont. After the death of her grandfather, in the early eighties, Sara's father takes over, expanding the company and creating the Belpaese consortium. In the nineties he receives the Knight of Labor medal from the President. The nightmare begins at the end of 2002. A clan of the 'ndrangheta, transplanted to Piedmont and operating throughout northern Italy, takes aim at the consortium. The construction sites are systematically vandalized, the materials and machines stolen, pressures are brought to bear on the suppliers, including blackmail and intimidation of every sort.

To avoid failure, Sara's father accepts the advice of his lawyer not to report what's happening to the police but, rather, to turn to the powerful men who control the territory. He discovers only later that the lawyer, too, was in the pay of the Calabrians. This is the first step on the road to hell. As time passes, members of the clan become partners in the business, inflate the accounts in order to launder dirty money, the product of illegal activities tied mainly to drugs. In the end Cavalier Bertini becomes simply a figurehead under the control of the clan. It's as if he didn't exist. Now he lives on antidepressant drugs. He is afraid of the consequences. Sooner or later everything will come to light. In recent years Sara's two brothers and her cousin have taken his place, and have become perfectly integrated into the new reality. They have no intention of protesting, in fact they try to profit from the situation. They keep saying: it's what all businessmen are doing, within the system or outside it.

Sara has never accepted this situation and, following the arrest of Bernardo Provenzano last April, after forty years of hiding, she decided to rebel. His arrival at police headquarters in Palermo is unforgettable: people greeted the boss of bosses shouting, "Bastard!" It was an extraordinary moment. So it's not true that crime is invincible. We must not let down our guard but continue the battles of Giovanni Falcone, Paolo Borsellino, and many others. We must react with strength and courage.

Sara mentions with admiration Addiopizzo, the movement founded two years ago by young Sicilians in Palermo to fight the extortion racket. She spent months gathering material, exploring two paths, that of the priest Don Costantino and that of Professor Lanzino. It was a big risk to take the photographs that make up part of the file.

I confine myself to listening. What can I say? You're great, congratulations, you were right to rebel. Good luck in your future life as a collaborator with justice. I don't know, she must have thought carefully before making this leap. I decide to silence, at least for the moment, my defeatism, my incurable pessimism.

"Enzo, we can't live in fear. You remember what Paolo Borsellino said?"

"One who is afraid dies every day."

"Exactly. Did you read the file?"

"Yes."

"When do you think you'll publish it?"

"The editor of the paper doesn't want to know about it. He said we can't be spoilsports."

"Really?"

"I'm sorry, Sara."

"Don't worry, Enzo. I already have a plan B."

"You'll go to another paper?"

"No, it's a waste of time. I've been in contact with a judge. I think the moment has come to hand the file over to the courts."

"But are you sure?"

We head out of the Valentino. I manage to extract a positive phrase: the courts are our last resort. Is it true? I don't know.

As we're crossing Corso Massimo d'Azeglio we see three guys coming toward us, they try to block us. We manage to escape by returning to the park. I know every corner of the Valentino, it's not easy to fool me. We emerge on the Corso Vittorio Emanuele side and run to Via Mazzini, looking behind us constantly. No one is following. We go into a bank, the safest place in the world. This unexpected event forces Sara to move up her plan B. She calls the judge she's been in touch with. After a few minutes a car arrives, with plainclothes police. We embrace each other, looking in each other's eyes, without saying a word.

In the late afternoon I get a call from my cousin Pietro with some very bad news. My mother felt ill this morning and was rushed to the hospital. The situation is serious; he didn't say anything else. I decide to leave immediately for Cosenza. Pietro had looked into flights before calling me, and luckily there's one from Turin to Lamezia Terme at five-thirty, and there are still seats. I don't have time to go home, I take a taxi to the airport. You never know with the traffic. During the drive ugly thoughts crowd my mind. I try to keep them at bay but I can't. One question obsesses me: what if my mother should die unexpectedly? I don't want to think of the consequences. But it would be the worst thing that could happen to me in this life. I lost my father twelve years ago. A tumor in his intestines killed him in six months. There was nothing to do. Chemotherapy was totally useless, it only increased his suffering.

I fly to Lamezia Terme and on my arrival I find not Pietro but his older brother Matteo. I haven't seen him for a couple of years. We've never been too fond of each other.

"Welcome! Did you have a good trip?" he asks me.

"How's Mamma?"

"She's fine."

"What hospital was she admitted to?"

"No hospital. She's at home."

"Pietro told me the situation was serious."

"It was a hoax, as you journalists say. An April fool's joke."

"What the fuck is going on?"

"Don't get upset."

"You want me to bash your face in?"

"Calm down! Your uncle wants to see you."

"You're a gang of fucking shits."

I fell for it like a fly in honey. But how could I have known? That shit Pietro, the boy father, was very good. A perfect performance. He'll pay for it. I call my mother to reassure myself that she's fine. She answers, a little astonished. She's always the one who calls. Always. I tell her I'm in Cosenza for work and I'll see her later. I try to calm down but with no luck. I smoke an MS.

"So where are we going."

"Enzo, I don't know."

"You're doing your best to make me lose patience."

"What I know is that I have to take you into town. Someone will take you to your uncle."

"Shits."

When we get there, Matteo hands me over to a guy with a van. And we depart. For where? It's pointless to ask. From my seat I can't see a thing, it's like being blindfolded. The same handing-over operation is repeated four times. Obviously they are precautions. Fugitives haven't been doing too well since Provenzano's arrest. The journey to my uncle's lasts a good three hours. Maybe we've only traveled in a circle, and haven't gone far at all. The hiding place could be in the center of the city. Finally we reach the destination. I'm in a garage connected to a house. They bring me into a small living room and tell me to wait. After ten minutes my uncle the boss arrives.

He's slightly changed; he has less hair. His body is the same, athletic and slender. He evidently spends a lot of time at the gym. I get up to greet him. I offer my hand, but he holds me in a strong embrace. We're alone.

"Here's my pain-in-the-ass nephew. How are you?"

"Fine."

"I know you're angry, but there was no other choice to get you here fast. We know your weak point. Eh, the mamma is the mamma."

"Why do you want to see me?"

"You're making quite a mess."

"For whom?"

My uncle is a taciturn type, he says and doesn't say, he leaves his interlocutor off balance. He's constantly sending coded messages. The certain thing is that he is skilled in diplomacy, it's his main talent. Recourse to violence is the final option. He begins his sermon on the importance of the family. He repeats stuff I've heard on many occasions: the extreme poverty during and after the Second World War, millions of Calabrians forced to emigrate, and blah blah blah. Then he talks about my father and how stubborn he was. Their roads divided, each made his own choices. Obviously one can't speak of the past without regrets and above all reproaches.

"Your father could become a boss, instead he chose to be the servant of the Agnellis."

"He did well."

"I seem to be talking to him," says my uncle.

"Like father, like son."

"Enzo, don't play with fire."

"I don't understand. What do you mean?"

"You understand perfectly. Stay away."

"From whom? Belpaese?"

"Very good."

"They're your partners?"

“You’re not here to interview me. Have I explained myself?”

“I just want to understand.”

“There’s nothing to understand. It’s better to occupy yourself with pigs.”

“I see that you are very well informed.”

“This time I managed to save your ass, the next time maybe I won’t be there.”

“I didn’t ask anyone for help.”

“Enzo, you still have time to move to the side of the bosses.”

“Uncle, you can’t put a square peg in a round hole.”

Acknowledgments

Places are important in my novels: Piazza Vittorio, Viale Marconi, San Salvario. In fact, they have the same weight as the characters. I think it would be fitting to pay homage to all the places that have welcomed me and inspired me during the writing of this novel. I would like to thank Anguillara, Berlin, Bracciano, Brighton, Michigan, Marseilles, Molbourne, Turin, and, obviously San Salvario, where I lived at the time.

I would also like to thank Irene Agnello, Daniela Brogi, Malvina Cagna, Michele Campanini, Chiara Carrer, Daniele Castellani Pirelli, Claudio Ceciarelli, Mirella and Roberto De Angelis, Giancarlo De Cataldo, Fabio Ferrero, Sandro Ferri, Massimiliano Fiorucci, Margherita Ganeri, Armando Gnisci, Elise Gruau, Francesco Leggio, Stephanie Love, Cristina Mauceri, Federica Mazzara, Viorica Nechifor, Grazia Nigro, Sandra Ozzola, Annalisa Pallotti, Viviana Pansa, Gerardo Papalia, Anna Pastore, Ferruccio Pastore, Emanuele Ragnisco, Maria Lella Rebecchini, Claudio Rossi, Grace Russo Bullaro, Alessandro Tarsia, and my friends at E/O.

About the Author

Amara Lakhous was born in Algiers in 1970. His first novel, *Clash of Civilizations Over an Elevator in Piazza Vittorio* (Europa Editions, 2008), was awarded Italy's prestigious Flaiano prize and was praised by the *Seattle Times* as a "wonderfully offbeat novel." He is also the author of *Divorce Islamic Style*.

www.europaeditions.com

EUROPA EDITIONS BACKLIST
(alphabetical by author)

Fiction

Carmine Abate
Between Two Seas • 978-1-933372-40-2 • Territories: World
The Homecoming Party • 978-1-933372-83-9 • Territories: World

Milena Agus
From the Land of the Moon • 978-1-60945-001-4 • Ebook • Territories: World (excl. ANZ)

Salwa Al Neimi
The Proof of the Honey • 978-1-933372-68-6 • Ebook • Territories: World (excl UK)

Simonetta Agnello Hornby
The Nun • 978-1-60945-062-5 • Territories: World

Daniel Arsand
Lovers • 978-1-60945-071-7 • Ebook • Territories: World

Jenn Ashworth
A Kind of Intimacy • 978-1-933372-86-0 • Territories: US & Can

Beryl Bainbridge
The Girl in the Polka Dot Dress • 978-1-60945-056-4 • Ebook • Territories: US

Muriel Barbery
The Elegance of the Hedgehog • 978-1-933372-60-0 • Ebook • Territories: World (excl. UK & EU)
Gourmet Rhapsody • 978-1-933372-95-2 • Ebook • Territories: World (excl. UK & EU)

Stefano Benni
Margherita Dolce Vita • 978-1-933372-20-4 • Territories: World
Timeskipper • 978-1-933372-44-0 • Territories: World

Romano Bilenchi
The Chill • 978-1-933372-90-7 • Territories: World

Kazimierz Brandys
Rondo • 978-1-60945-004-5 • Territories: World

Alina Bronsky
Broken Glass Park • 978-1-933372-96-9 • Ebook • Territories: World
The Hottest Dishes of the Tartar Cuisine • 978-1-60945-006-9 • Ebook • Territories: World

Jesse Browner
Everything Happens Today • 978-1-60945-051-9 • Ebook • Territories: World (excl. UK & EU)

Francisco Coloane
Tierra del Fuego • 978-1-933372-63-1 • Ebook • Territories: World

Rebecca Connell
The Art of Losing • 978-1-933372-78-5 • Territories: US

Laurence Cossé
A Novel Bookstore • 978-1-933372-82-2 • Ebook • Territories: World
An Accident in August • 978-1-60945-049-6 • Territories: World (excl. UK)

Diego De Silva
I Hadn't Understood • 978-1-60945-065-6 • Territories: World

Shashi Deshpande
The Dark Holds No Terrors • 978-1-933372-67-9 • Territories: US

www.europaeditions.com

Steve Erickson
Zeroville • 978-1-933372-39-6 • Territories: US & Can
These Dreams of You • 978-1-60945-063-2 • Territories: US & Can

Elena Ferrante
The Days of Abandonment • 978-1-933372-00-6 • Ebook • Territories: World
Troubling Love • 978-1-933372-16-7 • Territories: World
The Lost Daughter • 978-1-933372-42-6 • Territories: World

Linda Ferri
Cecilia • 978-1-933372-87-7 • Territories: World

Damon Galgut
In a Strange Room • 978-1-60945-011-3 • Ebook • Territories: USA

Santiago Gamboa
Necropolis • 978-1-60945-073-1 • Ebook • Territories: World

Jane Gardam
Old Filth • 978-1-933372-13-6 • Ebook • Territories: US
The Queen of the Tambourine • 978-1-933372-36-5 • Ebook • Territories: US
The People on Privilege Hill • 978-1-933372-56-3 • Ebook • Territories: US
The Man in the Wooden Hat • 978-1-933372-89-1 • Ebook • Territories: US
God on the Rocks • 978-1-933372-76-1 • Ebook • Territories: US
Crusoe's Daughter • 978-1-60945-069-4 • Ebook • Territories: US

Anna Gavalda
French Leave • 978-1-60945-005-2 • Ebook • Territories: US & Can

Seth Greenland
The Angry Buddhist • 978-1-60945-068-7 • Ebook • Territories: World

Katharina Hacker
The Have-Nots • 978-1-933372-41-9 • Territories: World (excl. India)

Patrick Hamilton
Hangover Square • 978-1-933372-06-8 • Territories: US & Can

James Hamilton-Paterson
Cooking with Fernet Branca • 978-1-933372-01-3 • Territories: US
Amazing Disgrace • 978-1-933372-19-8 • Territories: US
Rancid Pansies • 978-1-933372-62-4 • Territories: USA

Alfred Hayes
The Girl on the Via Flaminia • 978-1-933372-24-2 • Ebook • Territories: World

Jean-Claude Izzo
The Lost Sailors • 978-1-933372-35-8 • Territories: World
A Sun for the Dying • 978-1-933372-59-4 • Territories: World

Gail Jones
Sorry • 978-1-933372-55-6 • Territories: US & Can

Ioanna Karystiani
The Jasmine Isle • 978-1-933372-10-5 • Territories: World
Swell • 978-1-933372-98-3 • Territories: World

Peter Kocan
Fresh Fields • 978-1-933372-29-7 • Territories: US, EU & Can
The Treatment and the Cure • 978-1-933372-45-7 • Territories: US, EU & Can

Helmut Krausser
Eros • 978-1-933372-58-7 • Territories: World

Amara Lakhous
Clash of Civilizations Over an Elevator in Piazza Vittorio • 978-1-933372-61-7 • Ebook • Territories: World
Divorce Islamic Style • 978-1-60945-066-3 • Ebook • Territories: World

www.europaeditions.com

Lia Levi
The Jewish Husband • 978-1-933372-93-8 • Territories: World

Valerio Massimo Manfredi
The Ides of March • 978-1-933372-99-0 • Territories: US

Leïla Marouane
The Sexual Life of an Islamist in Paris • 978-1-933372-85-3 • Territories: World

Lorenzo Mediano
The Frost on His Shoulders • 978-1-60945-072-4 • Ebook • Territories: World

Sélim Nassib
I Loved You for Your Voice • 978-1-933372-07-5 • Territories: World
The Palestinian Lover • 978-1-933372-23-5 • Territories: World

Amélie Nothomb
Tokyo Fiancée • 978-1-933372-64-8 • Territories: US & Can
Hygiene and the Assassin • 978-1-933372-77-8 • Ebook • Territories: US & Can

Valeria Parrella
For Grace Received • 978-1-933372-94-5 • Territories: World

Alessandro Piperno
The Worst Intentions • 978-1-933372-33-4 • Territories: World
Persecution • 978-1-60945-074-8 • Ebook • Territories: World

Lorcan Roche
The Companion • 978-1-933372-84-6 • Territories: World

Boualem Sansal
The German Mujahid • 978-1-933372-92-1 • Ebook • Territories: US & Can

Eric-Emmanuel Schmitt
The Most Beautiful Book in the World • 978-1-933372-74-7 • Ebook • Territories: World
The Woman with the Bouquet • 978-1-933372-81-5 • Ebook • Territories: US & Can

Angelika Schrobsdorff
You Are Not Like Other Mothers • 978-1-60945-075-5 • Ebook • Territories: World

Audrey Schulman
Three Weeks in December • 978-1-60945-064-9 • Ebook • Territories: US & Can

James Scudamore
Heliopolis • 978-1-933372-73-0 • Ebook • Territories: US

Luis Sepúlveda
The Shadow of What We Were • 978-1-60945-002-1 • Ebook • Territories: World

Paolo Sorrentino
Everybody's Right • 978-1-60945-052-6 • Ebook • Territories: US & Can

Domenico Starnone
First Execution • 978-1-933372-66-2 • Territories: World

Henry Sutton
Get Me out of Here • 978-1-60945-007-6 • Ebook • Territories: US & Can

Chad Taylor
Departure Lounge • 978-1-933372-09-9 • Territories: US, EU & Can

Roma Tearne
Mosquito • 978-1-933372-57-0 • Territories: US & Can
Bone China • 978-1-933372-75-4 • Territories: US

André Carl van der Merwe
Moffie • 978-1-60945-050-2 • Ebook • Territories: World (excl. S. Africa)

Fay Weldon
Chalcot Crescent • 978-1-933372-79-2 • Territories: US

Anne Wiazemsky
My Berlin Child • 978-1-60945-003-8 • Territories: US & Can

Jonathan Yardley
Second Reading • 978-1-60945-008-3 • Ebook • Territories: US & Can

Edwin M. Yoder Jr.
Lions at Lamb House • 978-1-933372-34-1 • Territories: World

Michele Zackheim
Broken Colors • 978-1-933372-37-2 • Territories: World

Alice Zeniter
Take This Man • 978-1-60945-053-3 • Territories: World

Tonga Books

Ian Holding
Of Beasts and Beings • 978-1-60945-054-0 • Ebook • Territories: US & Can

Sara Levine
Treasure Island!!! • 978-0-14043-768-3 • Ebook • Territories: World

Alexander Maksik
You Deserve Nothing • 978-1-60945-048-9 • Ebook • Territories: US, Can & EU (excl. UK)

Thad Ziolkowski
Wichita • 978-1-60945-070-0 • Ebook • Territories: World

Crime/Noir

Massimo Carlotto
The Goodbye Kiss • 978-1-933372-05-1 • Ebook • Territories: World
Death's Dark Abyss • 978-1-933372-18-1 • Ebook • Territories: World
The Fugitive • 978-1-933372-25-9 • Ebook • Territories: World
Bandit Love • 978-1-933372-80-8 • Ebook • Territories: World
Poisonville • 978-1-933372-91-4 • Ebook • Territories: World

Giancarlo De Cataldo
The Father and the Foreigner • 978-1-933372-72-3 • Territories: World

Caryl Férey
Zulu • 978-1-933372-88-4 • Ebook • Territories: World (excl. UK & EU)
Utu • 978-1-60945-055-7 • Ebook • Territories: World (excl. UK & EU)

Alicia Giménez-Bartlett
Dog Day • 978-1-933372-14-3 • Territories: US & Can
Prime Time Suspect • 978-1-933372-31-0 • Territories: US & Can
Death Rites • 978-1-933372-54-9 • Territories: US & Can

Jean-Claude Izzo
Total Chaos • 978-1-933372-04-4 • Territories: US & Can
Chourmo • 978-1-933372-17-4 • Territories: US & Can
Solea • 978-1-933372-30-3 • Territories: US & Can

Matthew F. Jones
Boot Tracks • 978-1-933372-11-2 • Territories: US & Can

Gene Kerrigan
The Midnight Choir • 978-1-933372-26-6 • Territories: US & Can
Little Criminals • 978-1-933372-43-3 • Territories: US & Can

Carlo Lucarelli
Carte Blanche • 978-1-933372-15-0 • Territories: World
The Damned Season • 978-1-933372-27-3 • Territories: World
Via delle Oche • 978-1-933372-53-2 • Territories: World

Edna Mazya
Love Burns • 978-1-933372-08-2 • Territories: World (excl. ANZ)

Yishai Sarid
Limassol • 978-1-60945-000-7 • Ebook • Territories: World (excl. UK, AUS & India)

Joel Stone
The Jerusalem File • 978-1-933372-65-5 • Ebook • Territories: World

Benjamin Tammuz
Minotaur • 978-1-933372-02-0 • Ebook • Territories: World

Non-fiction

Alberto Angela
A Day in the Life of Ancient Rome • 978-1-933372-71-6 • Territories: World • History

www.europaeditions.com

Helmut Dubiel
Deep In the Brain: Living with Parkinson's Disease • 978-1-933372-70-9 • Ebook • Territories: World • Medicine/Memoir

James Hamilton-Paterson
Seven-Tenths: The Sea and Its Thresholds • 978-1-933372-69-3 • Territories: USA • Nature/Essays

Daniele Mastrogiacomo
Days of Fear • 978-1-933372-97-6 • Ebook • Territories: World • Current affairs/Memoir/Afghanistan/Journalism

Valery Panyushkin
Twelve Who Don't Agree • 978-1-60945-010-6 • Ebook • Territories: World • Current affairs/Memoir/Russia/Journalism

Christa Wolf
One Day a Year: 1960-2000 • 978-1-933372-22-8 • Territories: World • Memoir/History/20th Century

Children's Illustrated Fiction

Altan
Here Comes Timpa • 978-1-933372-28-0 • Territories: World (excl. Italy)
Timpa Goes to the Sea • 978-1-933372-32-7 • Territories: World (excl. Italy)
Fairy Tale Timpa • 978-1-933372-38-9 • Territories: World (excl. Italy)

Wolf Erlbruch
The Big Question • 978-1-933372-03-7 • Territories: US & Can
The Miracle of the Bears • 978-1-933372-21-1 • Territories: US & Can
(with **Gioconda Belli**) *The Butterfly Workshop* • 978-1-933372-12-9 • Territories: US & Can